23 3⁰⁰

THE SAMURAI

Rafael Reyes-Ruiz

First printing

ISBN: 978-0-578-58433-1

Published by LCG Media

Printed in the United States of America

Suggested Retail Price (SRP) $10.95

Cover and Design by Yanina Spizzirri

The Samurai is printed in Garamond

Praise for *The Samurai*

For readers interested in discovering the new horizons in Latin American and Latino literature, *The Samurai* and the trilogy to which it belongs clearly show that Latin American and Latino novels have crossed borders to engage other worlds.

—Juan Ryusuke Ishikawa, California State University, Fullerton.

Through an intimate first-person perspective, *The Samurai* explores migration as a phenomenon motivated by existential factors rather than economics. This novel approach is much needed to conversations and debates about immigration in the current political climate.

—Rubén Varona, Miami University, Ohio

Although each of the novels in the trilogy stands on its own, *The Samurai* pleasantly traps you in a labyrinth of existential questions about some of its recurrent characters and makes you want to return to read the first two.

—Shigeko Mato, Waseda University, Tokyo, Japan

The Samurai is a novel that says more than it seems on a first reading. Apart from its literary value, it reveals the real-life dangers some of the characters encounter behind ambiguous facades.

—Pilar Chargoñia, Universidad de la República, Uruguay

Special thanks to Colleen Quigley, Gonzalo Robledo, Robert Garot, Anke Reichenbach, Patrick O'Connor, Sandra Guerrero, June Carolyn Erlick, Kathleen DeSimone, and Pilar Chargoñia.

PART ONE

ONE

The gathering was at Lisa's house. An invitation came by way of a postcard—an old photo of Chinatown, signed by Veronique, my ex-girlfriend and now the informal leader of our group—reminding us that September 26 was the first anniversary of that night in the dining room at the Ansonia in downtown San Francisco, a youth hostel housed in a grand old Edwardian building that had seen better days, when over a few beers, all of us newcomers to town had promised to look after one another and remain friends. I had been a little distant from the group lately; I needed to put order into my life. What little I earned teaching Spanish and doing translations was barely enough for me to make ends meet.

The evening was cool and breezy, and the moonless sky was covered in a blanket of clouds. The small and narrow house on a hilly North Beach street was Mediterranean style with a pink stucco facade. In the back, overlooking the bay, it had a wooden terrace.

We were all there, some sitting in wicker chairs, others standing in a circle, reminiscing about our times at the Ansonia.

Although I was more or less aware of the group's goings-on through Veronique, who called me from time to time, I was surprised by how normal our lives now seemed, something that would not have occurred to any of us during those first few months in the city, of which all I remember is a constant steady drizzle and the frustration of not finding a job. I felt comfortable in the group but without the enthusiasm of the Ansonia days, especially of our after-dinner gatherings, the only thing that lifted my spirits and gave me hope.

At the beginning, we were three: Veronique and I, who arrived on the same day, and Lydia, who had been in the city for two weeks, also from Bordeaux like Veronique, who came for a year to work as an au pair and improve her English. The weekly rate at the Ansonia included dinner, making it easy to make friends with the other guests. A week later we met another: Felipe, a tall, burly Mexican architect who always seemed to be fleeing from somewhere. Lisa, who was from Chicago and had just spent two years teaching English in Seoul, invited herself to the group one night when we were about to go out for a beer at a bar nearby. The last person who joined was Elena, a Californian artist older than all of us—thirty or thirty-five—who did the afternoon shift at the Ansonia's front desk and seemed to have no friends in town.

Although it promised to be a fun, entertaining evening, I suddenly felt somewhat melancholy for the passing of time that relentlessly pulled me away from my friends with whom I shared so much not so long ago. I no longer felt so light, so optimistic, so ready for anything, and I had the vague feeling that I would not see them again after tonight, that our lives were going to take different paths. With that in mind, I went to the kitchen to get a beer; the glass of water I was holding in my hand was only a ploy for not drinking as fast as my friends. As I was coming back I ran into Elena, an empty beer bottle in her hand, and I felt that she had followed me on purpose so we could talk a little. Between us there was often an unfinished conversation, always interrupted by our friends, who liked to talk as if they were at a round table. The last time we had some alone time to talk was the day before I left when we met in the dining room before mealtime and discovered that we both had a passion for art films and detective novels.

You don't come by the hotel anymore, she said and indicated with her eyes we should go back to the kitchen.

That night Elena wasn't wearing her long blue-dyed hair loose as usual, but had it pulled up into a crown bun that made her look slightly taller than me. I told her I had a difficult schedule, but right away I realized that I should explain myself better. My classes are all over the city, I said. At private schools and with some lawyers. To be honest, downtown depresses me a little. When I go by, I feel as if I have lived there a long time, a kind of a lifetime sentence walking those streets up and down, downcast and unemployed.

Elena looked at me in silence and took a beer from the fridge. I think I know what you mean, she said, and sat across from me at the kitchen table. Can I tell you a story, and then you go back to what you were saying?

Sure, I said. It was Elena's style to ask permission to tell a story; that's how we knew about her life.

I lived in downtown for many years, she said and lit a cigarette. Not far from the Ansonia, on the same street, actually. It was a small apartment on the ground floor, and a bit dark. My mom worked at a fancy hotel in Union Square, and I went to school on the other side of Market Street, so I had to walk through downtown every day. I used to complain because I didn't like the crowded streets full of adults, and I would make a face. Mom would get mad and say: *You walk like a suffering soul, girl. If you're not careful, you're going to stay like that forever!*

Elena said these last two sentences in Spanish so

naturally that at first I did not realize she had switched languages. I asked her if she spoke Spanish, more by reflex than anything else; I had not thought it possible. I knew Elena was half Japanese, more because of what she once told us, rather than because of her looks; she didn't have Asian features. Almost the opposite—she had large, almost round eyes.

Of course, I speak Spanish, Ricardo, she said. Didn't you know that my mother is Mexican?

No, I said. I thought your last name, Ruggiero, was from your Italian mother.

Well, you missed that conversation, then, she said rather mockingly in English. I remember telling the story one night at the Ansonia. Perhaps you were distracted or were already gone. But you're right about something: my mother is of Italian origin, but very far back and only on my grandfather's side. And, by the way, my Spanish is horrible, so don't ever put me in an embarrassing situation.

Don't worry; I wouldn't do that. In that moment, and for the first time, I felt very attracted to Elena. Not because of what she said, but by the way she said it, which made me feel very close, as if we were intimate from way back. Right after that, it occurred to me that Elena wanted to be with me, to be my girlfriend or my lover or something like that. I was sure and confident of it, as when one instinctively knows which path to follow. It had not occurred to me until then that we could be a couple. Besides thinking that Elena was much older than I—ten years, even—I had imagined there was a deep chasm between us, something essential, of a practical nature, although I had not stopped to think what it would be. So far she had seemed a little conceited, especially when she talked about art and about her painting; she sounded as if she were teaching a class, saying this and that about other artists, sometimes making disparaging comments as if she were a well-known artist and beyond good and evil.

Tell me about that lifetime sentence, she said, again rather jokingly, and took a long sip of her drink.

I don't know how to explain it better, I said. It's the only image that comes to mind. It's like a never-ending punishment, in which everything is repeated, going around the same streets, in a vicious circle.

Veronique walked into the kitchen then. She said she came for a beer and went straight to the fridge. Behind her came Felipe, patted me on the arm, and stood beside me.

You guys look very serious, he said. What's the topic?

I heard something about going up and down the streets, Veronique said.

Elena laughed and said, Well, the night is young. What if we go to the blues bar?

Where Felipe declared his love to Lydia? asked Lisa, who had heard Elena from the hallway and came into the kitchen now.

Felipe shrugged and said that in his recollection it had been the other way around. Veronique burst out laughing, and said it would be best to ask Lydia, but she would probably not remember it either. In the end, the affair only lasted a week, so I fully understand that you'd want to forget it, she added with a smile from ear to ear.

The comment made us all laugh. We had witnessed the failed romance that began and ended without much ado and occasionally brought it up, but we would always tell them that we loved them, either as a couple or by themselves.

When we left the house, Elena took my hand in hers and laced her fingers with mine. There was nothing unusual about holding hands among us like that, even if we were not couples. Lydia and Veronique always started it, but Elena was quick to do it, and we walked quickly ahead so we could talk some more. I felt a kind of peace at that moment, as if all the tension of the week was fading away. I was doing some translations for a group of student lawyers, a lawsuit against a multinational oil company in Ecuador, and the difficulty of the documents had kept me up a couple of nights.

Elena looked relaxed and cheerful. She told me that she loved the neighborhood, the bohemian vibe, and the small Italian cafes and restaurants, and always wanted to live there, though she could hardly afford the the rent.

The night was getting a bit cold, and there was a sharp breeze that burst back and forth along the street. We walked noisily down the steep sloping street, the echo of our footsteps bouncing off the walls of buildings and houses. Veronique and Lisa were behind us, also holding hands, they looked like twins, both the same height, today sporting the same hairstyle, whispering something quietly.

On the second corner, one block before Columbus Avenue, the main drag of North Beach, a limousine was parked close to the curb, and beside it a scooter. The limo and the scooter drivers spoke quietly, but I realized it was in Spanish; I could hear the limo driver say, Nothing happened; you're very lucky. Don't worry, just go. At the corner, two men were talking, their backs to the drivers. One of them wore a trench coat with the collar turned up, which made me think of Alain Delon as the gun for hire in *The Samurai*. The man turned to us for a moment, and by his profile I realized he was

Asian—Korean or Japanese, Chinese perhaps—and in his sixties; he was tall and thin, with thick and somewhat bristling gray hair. While he spoke, he shook his left hand, the thumb and index fingers extended, in the right hand a cigarette, which he also shook slightly. When we passed by them, Elena looked sideways for a long while. I was going to say something, but Felipe joined us and said he was going to buy cigarettes, and would we please order a double whiskey for him.

There was a band playing at the bar, and luckily we found a large table in the back, next to the bar, across from the stage. The musicians said they were going to play "You Shook Me" by Muddy Waters to finish the set, and Lisa asked us all to dance, that it was her favorite song, and the waitress had agreed to keep their table. Elena said she would rather dance later, but because she was ahead of me, I told her it was too late, and with my hands on her shoulders, I pushed her lightly toward the dance floor. We started to couple dance, and at some point she kissed my cheek. In that instant, I was sure we were going to be a couple, and we'd get along very well. Veronique, who was dancing with Lisa, and perhaps had been looking at us for a while, winked at me and, with her hand, indicated that we should talk later.

When we sat at the table, Elena and I chose chairs

in front of the window, facing the street. Veronique sat on the other side of Elena and started talking with her about something that seemed important because a moment later, Elena turned toward me and gave me a half smile, a gesture I knew she made when something annoyed her, and I understood to also mean that we would later retake the thread we were weaving.

Felipe, sitting next to me, told me he was planning to return to Mexico; he missed his family.

Doesn't it happen to you, compadre? he asked.

No, I said, not in the least. As I mentioned before, I have a dysfunctional family. I told him that I had decided to become a citizen and had the naturalization exam next month.

A poco, great, he said, and gave me a half hug. Give me your guy's number?

It's a she, I said. At a nonprofit. It won't be hard to find her, I added. I'm not sure you qualify because you've gone back several times, right?

Felipe said yes, that maybe his case would be very difficult, if he had a case at all. Then he added, that's life and drank what remained of his whiskey in one go. The music started again, and Lisa and Lydia came to our side of the table to ask us to dance. Elena was still talking to Veronique; I thought it would have to be something serious. Elena looked concentrated, her forehead wrinkled.

Felipe said he would dance to anything and took my arm to follow him. We danced awhile, though I kept my eye on Elena and Veronique. I was hoping Elena would look my way for a moment so I could signal her to come join me, but she was still focused on the conversation. A few more minutes went by, and the dance floor filled with more young people like us and some older hippies. At some point, I saw Elena stand up. She looked out the window, distracted by something. Then she turned around, and our eyes met. She gestured that she was going to smoke a cigarette and stepped out.

I went back to the table with Lisa who, on seeing Veronique said, What happened? You look upset. Nothing, she said. I don't feel good, that's all. I don't know what's come over me.

The musicians kept playing, now a slower number, with a guitar solo. A new singer, an African American woman who had been alone in the bar, having a beer, took to the stage and began to moan following the melody. Lydia and Veronique now spoke French; I could understand that Veronique wanted to go home, that she was sorry, that she didn't want to spoil the evening.

You want us to keep you company? I asked.

Veronique gave me a half smile and said no, she

would take a taxi.

Say goodbye to Elena for me, she added. I looked out the window, thinking Elena was still smoking in the street, and then at the other side of the table, but she was not there. I don't know why but I had a hunch that something was wrong. Perhaps Veronique and Elena had quarreled. It occurred to me it was because of me—a rather stupid idea, I realized instantly, because neither of them was so petty. I looked around to make sure that Elena was not inside and ran into the street to look for her.

It was not more than ten minutes since she left, I calculated. I looked around everywhere, but I didn't see her. The bar was at a corner in a residential pocket, so I also looked on the cross street that went up toward Coit Tower, perched on top of Telegraph Hill, and tonight aglow in orange light. Felipe came after me and asked me what happened.

Call her cell phone, I said. I forgot mine.

It rang three times, and then it was disconnected, Felipe said after a few moments.

I walked to Columbus Avenue, where there was a lot of traffic at that time. I felt devastated. People passed by me, all strangers, some with happy or serious faces, others just indifferent. A black limousine drove by, suddenly accelerating. One of the passengers opened the window and threw a cigarette butt in the street. I suddenly remembered when Elena had looked over the Asian man with the trench coat, an hour ago, perhaps. I remembered that Elena was half-Japanese and had never met her father. I thought that that was why she had looked that way; perhaps she had thought her father would be a man that age. Perhaps there was something else, something I could not guess at the time. That's how my life was in the city so far. I had horrible luck; the worst things happened to me. I didn't know what the hell was happening with my life.

This is not a time to feel sorry for myself, I thought.

TWO

Elena answered the phone and said hello, how are you? in a casual tone, as if nothing had happened last night.

We were very worried about you, I said and added nothing; I let her fill the silence so that she would explain herself. I knew nothing serious had happened because Felipe called in the morning to tell me that Elena had sent a text saying everything was fine, to please excuse her.

I decided to call that afternoon because I thought she would not take the initiative.

After a long moment, Elena said it was complicated; everything was com-pli-ca-ted. Perhaps it was better that we talk face-to-face. What if you come by the hotel tonight?

I'm not sure I have the time, I replied. Why don't you tell me what's complicated? Do you need to see me for that?

My head is spinning, Ricardo. I was going to call in

a little while, believe me. Have you talked to Veronique?

I don't want to talk to Veronique. I'm fed up with her problems.

Well, you'll learn what this is about soon enough. That aside, something weird happened to me last night. Not with you. I also want to talk about us, but not now. Last night, I saw something that upset me, and I didn't know what to do but go home. I'll tell you everything when I see you, OK?

We met in the lobby of the Ansonia and went to a small Japanese sushi restaurant up Powell Street, toward Nob Hill. Elena insisted on treating me; she said it was the least she could do to apologize.

Veronique wants to stay in the United States, she told me, as we sat at a table, facing the street. I know that you know, but you may not be aware of what's happened recently. I tell you this because you'll find out soon, she said, and cleared her throat. The air in the room was very dry because of the heating.

She wants me to marry her for the papers, I said, looking at her in the eye.

Aha, she exclaimed. You both had planned it.

We had thought about it when we were dating, I said. But, you know how she is. Later, she said that this was not a country for her, that she had her job and her place in Bordeaux, and so on and so forth.

Lisa and Veronique are a couple now, Ricardo. That's why Veronique wants to stay.

Veronique and Lisa?

For a month or so now. Veronique told me last night. She's very much in love; she says it feels like the real deal.

It doesn't surprise me they're a couple, but it does that Veronique wants to stay for that. She falls in love all the time: Lisa today, Felipe tomorrow, Lydia the day after.

Don't be so mean, Ricardo. This is serious. Forget your sarcasm for a moment, can you?

Elena sounded really angry; she took her head in her hands and with her fingers rubbed her temples. You'll have to figure out how to deal with this. She's your friend, and *our* friend, remember?

Of course, I said. But this complicates everything—we would have to live together and all that. You know how immigration is in this country.

Veronique told me you already talked about living together at your place, when your roommates leave. Elena said this in a slow voice. She sounded more relaxed now.

Yes, we talked about it. You're right. But it was an idea, nothing else; I never imagined it would be for real.

I thought Veronique was going to keep working part-time with the same family for another four months and then return to France.

Veronique lost her job, Elena said. Actually, she quit it, and she's now staying with Lisa.

Why didn't they tell us?

They were going to announce it later last night, when we were more relaxed, more mellow, Elena said, shrugging. My brilliant idea of going out changed everything; well, it delayed it a bit, really. Veronique will tell you all this tomorrow, I hope. I'm telling you now because Veronique asked me to talk to you, to prepare the ground, so to speak. According to her, you always listen to me.

I'd rather not think about that now, I said. My life is also a mess, you know.

Elena leaned back in her chair and looked at me askance, as if she doubted what she'd just heard. It was a typical gesture of hers, and sometimes it gave me the impression that she was a bit condescending, as if what she'd heard was silly or immature. I said nothing but held her gaze, though I suddenly felt uncomfortable. We were the only customers in the restaurant that Sunday night, and the waiters seemed to be watching us from the back of the room, as if we were on a sort of theater stage. I took a long sip of my beer and asked

Elena why she looked at me that way.

I think you're the sanest of all of us in the group, she said. Apart from Felipe, who is always wise and even-keeled, though quiet as a tomb.

Felipe may not talk with you that much, but we always have long conversations. What happens is that you intimidate him. His English is horrible, and you are always correcting everybody.

The food came then, and Elena again rubbed her temples.

I'm really sorry, Ricardo, she said when the waiter left. Last night was going great—until the chat with Veronique, of course. I was a little angry with her because I couldn't understand why she didn't go straight to you. I'll never understand what the deal is between you two; that's another kettle of fish altogether. But as I said before, what happened to me last night was something else.

Elena again leaned back in her chair, as if pausing to measure her words.

While I was talking to Veronique, I saw the two guys pass by through the window, the ones next to the limo and the scooter, remember?

The Asian guy who looked like a samurai gun for hire?

This is no joke, Ricardo. The guy reminded me of

my father for a second, just like that.

Didn't you tell me you've never met your father?

Well, I never really met him. My father abandoned us when I was three years old. I almost never think about it, but last night when I saw that man, something in his face, perhaps his expression, looked familiar. It's as if I'd recognized something in him that I see when I look at myself in the mirror.

You don't look at all like that man, I said.

Maybe not, but that's what I felt, so I went out to smoke a cigarette. I thought if I looked at him closely, something would happen, that he would recognize me.

Did you talk to him?

No, he was with his friend, and they were walking fast. They went down to Columbus Avenue and made a left. I thought they were going to go into one of the striptease joints—don't ask me why I thought that—but no, they walked past them. I quickened my step; I almost ran, but there were so many people that I lost them for a moment. They'd crossed the street toward the City Lights bookstore, and now the light was red. While waiting for the traffic signal to change, I got upset. I'd promised myself—and Mom too—that I'd never again fuck around with this business of my father. I crossed the street, and though I looked everywhere, I couldn't find them. I thought I'd go back to the club, but

I was really distressed and thought it was enough drama for one night.

While she recounted that, Elena wrinkled her forehead, as if she was again feeling the frustration she must have felt when she couldn't find the guy. It was odd that she and I had felt something similar the night before, a few blocks from each other.

Do you understand now why I went home without saying anything?

I nodded yes, and thought about telling her that something like that had also happened to me last night, but at that instant the image of the Asian man came to my mind: he was an older man but had no wrinkles on his face. Perhaps he had makeup on, I thought, and that's why he looked to me like Alain Delon, the gun-for-hire character in *The Samurai* movie.

You have pictures of your father? I asked.

No, and neither does Mom. Only an old newspaper clipping, where he is with a group of actors and movie people in a jazz club.

Don't tell me your father was an actor.

Mom says he was a crook who could act, but I've no idea whether he was an actor, a producer or a cameraman, only that he worked in the movie business. It's a sad story, and she doesn't like to talk about it; she gets angry if I ask anything about it. The only thing she says is that they didn't get along.

Elena stared absently into the street. She seemed to have lost her appetite and had barely touched her food.

You said you talked to Felipe last night? she asked, suddenly alert, as if she had found in the street the key to something.

I told her, yes, a little.

Did he say he took good pictures last night? When we went down the street from Lisa's house, he was taking pictures of something, perhaps of the houses—you know how he likes the architecture in the city—but when we got to the corner where the limo was and I turned to look at the guy, I don't remember seeing Felipe. Could he have been taking pictures?

I don't know. I could ask him. I understand what you're thinking. I'll call him.

Elena nodded her head.

Felipe let it ring twice before he answered his mobile. I explained the situation the best way I could without mentioning the story of Elena's father and asked about the photographs. Felipe said yes, though at that corner he'd taken pictures of the two of us from the other side of the street because we looked happy together, and then he had a good laugh. You're with her?

I said yes and asked whether he could send the

pictures to my cell.

The pictures came a few minutes later. In the best of them, I could only see Elena and me talking. It would have been a few moments after we saw the two men. The lighting was dim—the light from the lamppost was enough for us though not for the surroundings—and the only other thing visible was the back of the limo.

Elena said, What a shame, and she put her hand on her chin.

I showed the other three pictures, which were roughly the same, one, two, or three seconds later. Elena looked at them carefully.

We came out well, you and I, don't you think? she said and looked at me pointedly the way she'd done it the night before when we were going down the street hand in hand.

What are you doing tomorrow? Are you going to work early?

I start at ten, I said.

In that case, you stay with me, she said, and leaned back on her chair, smiling.

We went back to Market Street and took the tram to the Castro stop. From there we walked up the street, almost to the top of the hill. The sky was cloudy, and a fine drizzle began to fall, which made us walk faster.

I had never been to Elena's place. The one time she threw a party for the group, I couldn't come; it was the weekend when my father had his first heart attack, and I was glued to the phone for several nights. Besides, it coincided with the breakup with Veronique, which wasn't easy, especially for her.

When we came in, I had the impression of being in a haunted house. It was on the second floor of an imposing Victorian home with a yellow facade, and the lights were dimmed. Beyond the staircase was a long corridor decorated with several portraits, five or six, which seemed like old photos, but that turned out to be Elena's black-and-white paintings with a distinct Gothic feel to them in a sober style of imaginary characters, members of a distinguished family of the city. Elena said she did them in art school, but she no longer painted like that. I wanted to take a closer look, but Elena had me by the hand and would not let me stop.

The living room, in the back of the apartment, had windows that commanded the valley that lay below the Castro, which looked like a large multicolored nativity scene. Elena stopped and motioned with her eyes to contemplate the view. In the distance, you could see the green swath of Dolores Park, and—far beyond—a line of twinkling lights, the Bay Bridge to Oakland. Three lamps lit the room, but two of them had pieces of colored fabric over them to dim the light. The furnishings consisted of a large couch and three armchairs in blue velvet, two of which were occupied by two dozing brown tabbies with gray stripes.

Sit on the couch while I get us a beer, Elena said. My roommates went out tonight, and they'll be late, she added, going into the adjoining kitchen. The painting facing you is the latest I've done, and it's already sold; the buyer will come for it in a couple of days.

I looked where at first I had not noticed anything on the wall, and out of the relative darkness emerged a large oil painting of a kind of hurricane or whirlwind seen from afar, in dark grays with small spots and paint splatter in vivid colors, and in the upper corner a yellow stain like sunlight through a hole in the clouds.

Awesome, I said aloud. I like it.

You'd better, said Elena who came back and sat beside me. It is a sort of vision I've dreamed about several times: something huge that spins and spins and makes a lot of noise, throwing sparks and flashes of light. You don't think I'm crazy, do you?

I shook my head. I couldn't think what to say. I realized I was a little nervous. I was entering new ground and felt a kind of fear, perhaps unfounded, that I couldn't manage things well. It was not that Elena intimidated me; it was perhaps that I didn't have enough confidence in myself. Since our brief conversation at Lisa's, I had begun to feel that with Elena the stakes were high; I would have to take a big step, a sort of leap of faith that could hurt me in the long run, or it could be completely the opposite, and it would transform me into a more confident person, less afraid of living. The age difference did not bother me; on the contrary, it seemed to me a big advantage at the moment. It would be good for me to be with someone more mature and experienced, I thought. I don't know why, but at that moment an image of Elena as a little girl came to my mind, the one she'd described: a bad-tempered brat walking around downtown with her mother. At that age, I had been the opposite, submissive and quiet; it would not have occurred to me to complain about anything.

Look, Ricardo, Elena said, taking my hand and lacing her fingers in mine. Let's not talk about anything tonight, shall we? We'll smoke a joint and go to bed. We'll talk tomorrow, all right?

THREE

When I woke up, Elena was reading in bed. She glanced at me and took my hand by way of greeting. I had it stretched toward her. I asked her what she was reading.

Japanese art, she said, and showed me a cover of a book that had a painting of a young woman in manga style. Are you interested in things Japanese?

A little, in film, I said. The rest, I don't know much about. Practically nothing. Not many years ago, I read a novel by someone whose name I don't remember, a historical piece about Jesuit missionaries in Japan in the sixteenth century, I think. I tried to remember the author's name, but all that came to mind was our library at home in Bogotá.

Would you like to go to Japan some time? Elena asked. Something in her eyes and in her tone of voice told me that she was mulling this over.

Not for the moment, I said. It's a faraway land. Images of some Japanese movies that I'd seen recently, a train station in winter, a tax inspector's office, and some family scenes, came to mind, but I had not liked any of those works enough to talk about them. I've heard they don't like foreigners there. That some go there and disappear, I added. I finished saying this and realized that I'd said it almost by reflex; it was something I had not thought of recently.

How is this? Elena let go of my hand and gathered her hair in a ponytail, which she fastened with an elastic band.

Never mind that, I said. It's a story with missing parts; a piece of unconfirmed gossip that probably has an easy and logical explanation.

Even so, I'd like to know, she said and put the book aside.

I told her it was about a second cousin who had gone to Japan to work as a nurse the same year I came to the United States, and from whom no one had heard since.

Is it a true story, or one of your tall tales? At the Ansonia you had a reputation as a teller of tall stories, always recounting odd episodes about your eccentric family: the whims of your father who thinks himself an English aristocrat, and the love adventures of your older brother, the best ballroom dancer in the world, or something like that. Still frowning, Elena said this with a slight air of reproach, but more pretend that serious.

Those were jokes. With many grains of truth, but still jokes. You always were late to our gatherings, so you didn't get all the background information. Someday I'll tell you about my crazy family. What I said about my cousin is for real; though she's someone I don't know well.

Tell me anyway, Elena insisted. But let's eat something, she said, stretching her arms and getting up.

We went to the kitchen, which was now flooded with light that came through a sliding glass door that led to a terrace with a wooden balustrade like the one at Lisa's house. There were dishes draining next to the sink, and traces of a recent breakfast: the smell of coffee, jam and butter on the table. The wall clock showed ten past eight.

She's a cousin from my mom's side and comes from another city in another state, I said while Elena made us coffee and toast. I've met her only once or twice in my life; her name is Adriana. Five years ago, in 2001, one of her patients, a Japanese engineer who spent a week in the hospital where she worked, suggested she go to work at a private hospital for the elderly in Yokohama. I remember these details well because when my mother told us the story, my dad—always so arrogant and a Mr. know-it-all—said that the hospital business was bullshit, that to him it sounded like prostitution.

Elena suddenly turned around and looked at me with a shadow of concern, as if my father's suspicion was right on the money. It had not occurred to me it could be; in fact, I had not even thought about it. It was one of those things that someone tells you, but that you have no opinion on or take a side with because it doesn't concern you. Adriana was a distant cousin, on whom I once had a crush, though I had not thought about her in a long time. Mom had told us about the job offer as a piece of good news—it made no difference to me—and my dad's response was typical of him; he treated my mom's family with contempt because they were unassuming and poor. For him and for my brother, these distant relatives were only worthy of ridicule: their provincial accent and their way of talking, and their lack of *refinement*, which to my dad was a sort of mortal sin.

And then what happened? Elena asked and sat next to me.

I don't know. We didn't mention the topic again at home. I was preparing my trip at the time and was also in a crunch with my dad, who wanted me to do something else. I'll tell you the whole story some other time. Mom reminded me of this a few months ago on the phone. She said that they had not heard from Adriana, that they did at first, but that from one day to the next there was no more, that she stopped calling home. Mom and I talked about many things, and I didn't much care for that, so I didn't ask for any further explanation.

But you do know that these things happen, right?

That people are tricked into prostitution? Yes, of course, I've read something about that, I said, though I couldn't remember anything specific. Adriana *is* a nurse, I added. And, if I'm not mistaken, they sent her a work contract and the paperwork for a visa.

Another Japanese mystery, Elena said. Like my father.

Elena's face darkened then, and I remembered about the vertigo she had felt when she couldn't find the man she said resembled him.

I like your room, I said. The purple walls are great. What's the poster above the bed?

It is the famous *Fall of Icarus* by Brueghel, my favorite painting.

Icarus? The one with wax on his wings?

He falls from the sky on the right corner.

I didn't see that. How tragic.

Speaking of which, send me Felipe's pictures, will you?

When I returned to the kitchen, Elena had her laptop on the table.

Look what happens when I expand the photos, she said. In the corner of one of the photos the back of the limo was visible. Do you see the license plate?

It's a miracle, I said. You can see all the numbers.

It's all I need, she said and opened her Internet browser.

While Elena searched the Net, I walked around the living room. I felt at ease, even fantasized about what it would be like to live there. The apartment I shared with a couple of medical students near Golden Gate Park was comfortable, but very dark; the windows faced a row of leafy trees. Perhaps the lack of light was depressing me, I thought.

Next to the window there was a bookcase, and in it several books on Japan, mostly art history, but also culture, and in one corner, language. I took one from that last section, and saw it was for an advanced level. It was evident that Elena was a committed student because some pages had many notes: new sentences in Japanese written several times, surely to improve her writing in Chinese characters.

It's a company out of Oakland, Elena said out loud after a few minutes. I'll call them. Elena came into the living room, cell phone in hand, and sat in one of the armchairs. The brown tabbies I'd seen the night before were now playing with rag toys on the sofa.

Whoever answered the phone did not speak English well because Elena repeated her question several times. She wanted to contact one of their customers because he or she had forgotten some keys in a restaurant in North Beach and they've just realized the keys must have belonged to one of the limo's passengers. The conversation didn't improve after that because Elena frowned, insisted in many different ways, said goodbye, and threw the phone into the other chair.

We can't give any information, she said in a mock Asian accent.

The scooter was from a pizza restaurant delivery service in North Beach, I said. Napoletana, I added and was amazed at my visual memory.

So what?

The guy was Central American, Salvadoran perhaps.

Elena shrugged.

I heard him speak Spanish with the limo's driver. At the very least, he can tell us whether the other guy was also from El Salvador.

Elena called, and the manager who was also the owner, answered. She said she found a set of keys lying on the street in a corner near Columbus Avenue and saw a delivery service scooter take off. She said she wanted to locate the person riding the scooter to give back the keys in person. Elena got the words mixed up while saying that, but the person at the other end understood or didn't ask her to repeat anything, and said (Elena repeated phrases for me to hear), that it was possible that the keys belonged to the guy in charge of home deliveries, that he'd learned he'd had a fender-bender with a limousine for Japanese VIPs staying at the Nikko hotel, that perhaps he'd accidentally dropped the keys there, and that she could come by later that afternoon between five and six to return them, if they belonged to him.

I'll call the hotel, Elena said after hanging up the phone, but immediately said no, she had to think through things better. Help me, she said.

Just say that a middle-aged or older Japanese guy with salt-and-pepper hair forgot some keys at a restaurant or something.

The receptionist at the Nikko said they had many guests who fit that description and could give no further information; she could leave the keys with the reception, and the staff there would ask the guests.

I'm going to the Nikko in Japantown, she said the moment she hung up. Would you come with me?

That week the Nikko Hotel had several corporate events involving Japanese companies, part of a joint effort between the Japanese consulate and the San Francisco Chamber of Commerce to promote trade exchanges. In the lobby, there was a list of companies indicating where their stands were located in one of the large conference rooms.

Come, Elena said and took my hand. I think today is my lucky day.

There were at least twenty stands of all kinds of companies, mostly electronic, biotechnology, and food products. We went around the conference room a couple of times and lingered wherever we saw older men, but to Elena, none of the faces looked familiar. I didn't say anything because all men of the age and demeanor of the man I remembered seemed the same to me. After going around a few more times, Elena began taking pictures of the people standing nearby, as if she couldn't trust her ability to distinguish the man for herself and had to carefully go over the photos later.

Some of the companies had a space to meet potential customers or employees with a small table and chairs; some even had a small curtained enclosure, perhaps for job interviews. Without exception, all the representatives of the Japanese companies wore business suits, as did many of the visitors, men and women, and were mostly in their thirties or forties, some older. Elena and I were probably the only young people around and also the only ones dressed informally. One of the stands caught my attention precisely because of the contrast. I caught sight of a couple, young like us, but better dressed, requesting information or asking questions from an older balding Japanese man, and a younger one, of Mediterranean or Latin looks. Elena also took note of the place and beckoned me with her eyes to go there.

They look more relaxed, she said. Not so *corporate*. When the couple leaves, we could go ask them if they know or have seen a tall man with bristly hair. Help me think of a good story.

Stay with the story with the keys, I said. The less you complicate it the better.

Hemispheres, Elena said, reading the stand's sign. I wonder what kind of company it is.

The Japanese man looked very pleased to see us. I'm glad you came, he said. Let me guess: English and French?

Sorry? Elena's face blushed with the question, shook her head no, and told me with her eyes to give her a hand. The other man asked us what languages we taught.

English and Spanish, I said, and added quickly that that was not why we came.

We just wanted to ask about a businessman we need to find. It's a personal matter, I explained.

The Japanese man looked at us closely for a moment. What is it about? he asked and adjusted his tie.

Elena recounted as best as she could the story with the limo and the keys on the street, and described the man as in his sixties, with a youthful face, and bushy gray hair.

The two men looked at each other.

We don't know anyone like that, said the Japanese man, stammering a little. The staff at the reception could help you with this.

Elena looked a little bewildered and again took my hand. We were about to leave when the younger man spoke:

I won't take much of your time, he said and gave us a brochure with two business cards stapled on top. I see that you're in a hurry. We are a language school in Tokyo with branches in several Japanese cities, and in Korea, and we have several openings for teachers of English, Spanish, French, and other languages. If you are interested, come back soon, before Friday, and we'll give you further information.

The Japanese man shook his head in agreement as his colleague spoke.

Elena started to read the brochure. It occurred to me that she would be interested in a language school, that perhaps she had contemplated a job like that in the future. I remembered that on one occasion Elena asked Lisa several questions about her job teaching English in Seoul: If it was easy, if students were well behaved, how was the pay, and about other things that perhaps she imagined were similar in Japan.

Do you need to have experience? Elena asked suddenly, her eyes fixed on the brochure.

What's most important is the desire to share the language, the Japanese man said. The ideal requirements are a college degree and a language-teaching certificate, but our company is flexible when it comes to the certificate.

When we left the stand, Elena burst out laughing.

Did you see how the bald guy looked at me? One would say that I scared him.

Now what? I asked.

Elena took from her bag two keys on a keychain with the letters ER on it. You go to the reception and hand them these keys, she said. You say that your girlfriend called this morning; you know what I said. Then you go to work, right? I'll stick around, waiting for the samurai. I'll sit in the reception area and take pictures of whomever they show the keys to.

FOUR

Elena called while I was waiting for the bus.

Did you find the samurai? I asked.

No, and I don't know if I saw him. There were too many people in the hotel lobby. I saw several tall, gray-haired Japanese men, but none of them looked familiar to me. I took many pictures, and I'll take a closer look at them later, just in case. I have a headache now. Are you on your way home?

Yes, I said. I have an early morning class with the lawyers.

See you later, then, Elena said and left the phrase hanging in the air.

You want to meet tomorrow night? I asked and then felt bad for taking the initiative. I didn't want to give the impression of coming on too strong; I wanted Elena to feel comfortable with me.

Can you come over for dinner? Elena asked in an animated voice; maybe she was waiting for me to take the first step.

Sure, I said. I'm free after seven.

Good. Oh, you know what? I saw the Japanese and the Latino guy again. They were talking with one of the clerks at the reception for a long time. They both looked at me for a moment and waved. The Latino guy's name is Javier Pinto, according to his business card. Does that sound Mexican or Colombian to you?

He could be from anywhere, I said. I couldn't detect an accent. But the name reminds me of something. Does he write his name with an X or a J?

I'm not sure; let me see. With an X, she said. Why do you ask?

No reason, just curious, I said; then we hung up.

At the supermarket near home, I bought some things I needed and grabbed a few beers. While standing in line to pay, I thought my life was yet again going off course. In the last four months, I'd gotten used to being on my own, following my own pace with work, not having to think about other people's businesses, and now I was getting entangled with Elena and her problems.

There was no one at home. My roommates had the same night shift that semester at the university hospital, and I only saw them on weekend mornings. I had nothing in common with them except a taste for jazz, especially from the fifties and sixties—John Coltrane, Miles Davis, Charles Mingus—which they always played when they were at home. Their taste in films was horrible; they collected Hollywood blockbusters, but thanks to their schedule, I could enjoy the large flat-screen TV they had in the living room to watch my favorite movies.

While I ate my dinner, I thought how wonderful it was to spend the night with Elena. It had been a long time since I'd felt so free with another person; I'd allowed myself to be my own self, without worrying how other people saw me or whether I was behaving well and saying the right things at the right times. With Veronique, I'd always felt self-conscious and limited because she had the upper hand in our relationship. Although she often consulted me, it was she who decided what we did, where we went for dinner, what movie we saw. If we were with the group, it was she who told what we'd done, what had happened to us. When I recounted something, especially if it was something from my past, I had the impression that it bored her, or she found the topic inappropriate or distasteful; she said something like this more than once. Her obsession with the novel she claimed she was writing often ruined the time we spent together. She would spend hours taking notes in a leather-bound notebook she carefully kept locked in her backpack and wouldn't tolerate my asking any questions or disturbing her otherwise. On the only occasion we talked about it, she said she was a bit superstitious; she thought that talking about her book with others would somehow take her off course. She could only say that it was about the sensual experiences of a young woman who wants to live life to the fullest. Later, she explained—though I didn't ask—that her writings had nothing to do with our relationship, perhaps suggesting that her literature had a higher horizon, beyond anything that we might experience together.

As I thought about that, I began to feel angrier with her than I'd been in the afternoon. She'd come to see me at school during the half-hour break between my classes. She showed up at the gate just when I finished my four o'clock class. She knew well my Monday schedule; it had not changed since we were together. I told her straightaway that Elena had told me about her suggestion of us getting married for her visa; I wanted to get to the point and avoid her roundabout way of getting to things; Veronique sometimes talked in circles.

She was surprised and told me she'd not said that; then she corrected herself and said yes, but that it was an aside, a reference to a possible scenario where things would go smoothly, but the main point was her relationship with Lisa. Besides, didn't you tell me you would help me whether we were together or not? she asked, and I had to say yes; I couldn't think what else to say then, though it was a scenario I wanted to avoid.

I closed my eyes and tried to remember the time we talked about the prospect of getting married. If I wasn't mistaken, it came out of a sort of funny scenario about our relationship down the line that she came up with one night, in which each of us benefited from the nationality of the other: she could live in the United States and write her novels, and I could go to France for a few years where I would study film and be close to directors I admired. What an inane thought that had been! But we took it seriously then, because a little later, when we talked about how we would actually do it, we both agreed why not, no matter what, the world was unfair with all that business with borders and passports, and we'd laughed; perhaps we were drinking and toasted to it.

I suddenly remembered that we took many more photographs than usual during those days. Perhaps it was because of Veronique's birthday—she was twenty-five, a year younger than I—so I decided to check them carefully. I went to my room and opened my computer photo-editing program where I kept the pictures I took and the ones my friends sent me. There were a hundred or more; I'd not removed any lately. Most of them were from Veronique, who liked to document everything, as she used to say. Some of the others were Felipe's—mostly group shots he took from time to time and often without warning, some in black and white, others in color. The few others were mine and taken with my new camera, which also did videos.

I had not looked at the pictures for a while, especially the earlier ones, and I felt a bit nostalgic. There they were, my first few months in the city: with the group in the Ansonia's dining hall, the joy of friendship, my infatuation with Veronique, my attachment to her, our night escapades in Chinatown and North Beach, the empty streets on our way back nearly at dawn, our walks through Presidio Park, and the Marina district under San Francisco's intense Mediterranean light. Some were of colorful houses and buildings, but most were of us. I scrolled quickly from one to another, from the first to the last, like watching a movie. I stopped arbitrarily at one of a batch taken in the Ansonia's dining hall. It was toward the end of the file, more or less where I thought it would be my last weeks at the hotel, and the time of my breakup with Veronique.

It was a photo Felipe took in the dining room. Lisa and I on one side of the table, Lydia and Veronique in front. As if the images had a soundtrack, I remembered that Lydia was telling us about the terrorist attack in Spain that week; she was worried about friends in Madrid. In the next picture, from another angle, but farther away, I'm no longer at the table, or in the image, Lisa, Lydia, and Veronique are talking, their bodies stretched toward each other, as if they were sharing a secret. I expanded the picture and saw that my things were still on the table, my phone and my keys. I remembered that I'd gone out to buy some beer at the corner store. I was already working at school, maybe in my first or second week. I moved to the next picture, which was pretty much like the one before, though in this one Veronique is looking at the camera with bewilderment or surprise, and the picture is not very sharp; perhaps she suddenly moved. Right away, I realized that the day we talked about our marriage of convenience was much earlier, maybe a couple of weeks before; I'd not yet started to teach.

In the next picture, taken from a different angle, but closer, I'm already back at the table. It's also an unexpected picture because nobody is posing. It's later—after eight because Elena also appears; she's finished her shift at the reception. I expanded the image as much as I could to take a closer look at Elena. She was kitty-corner to me and was looking in my direction with a half smile. My face is not visible; it's hidden by Lisa's back, who is chatting with Lydia. I might have been talking to Elena then, I can't remember, but I feel it was so. Lisa and

Veronique are on the other side of the picture, deep in conversation; perhaps they were already flirting with each other.

I took a long look at the picture, and I thought the image would be a good starting point. In the script I would write for my first movie, Elena and I were lovers. Veronique, my girlfriend, didn't know; I want to tell her later when we are alone, but she doesn't give me a chance. The scenarios would be similar or the same, a student or backpacker hostel in a city in North America, and the characters in the film would be us, the group. Following that initial scene, there would be flashbacks of our relationship: the weekend we went camping in Bodega Bay, on the beach near where Hitchcock made some shots for *The Birds* and the night we were in Berkeley with my former college classmates, intermixed with scenes of the group, our best friends, who also try to find their way in this country, foreign to us all. The third and final part would consist of fragments of our quarrels and disagreements which, despite being relatively minor, lead to our breakup, the inevitable conclusion. The ending would be like the one of *Full Moon in Paris*, a film by Eric Rohmer, in which Louise, the protagonist, tells her boyfriend in a scene that foreshadows the end of their relationship, *Don't take it to heart; it's just the way I am*, to explain why she has to spend the weekends in the city with her friends. In my script, it is I who says that, and just like in the film, it's not clear that I really know myself; my life, like Louise's, is full of contradictions.

It's just the way I am, I repeated to myself. It was the worst cliché for such a delicate moment, but that's pretty much what I told Veronique, when moved by something I didn't understand at the time, and I still do not—apart from the fact that I was certain of it—I proposed to her that we break up, that it made no sense for us to go on together. By way of explanation, I told her that something in me had changed, knowing that it wouldn't add or explain anything, unable to say more for fear of hurting her. I didn't know what else to say. I thought of telling her that I felt suffocated, that I couldn't be myself with her, but I held back. I knew it wasn't that; it would be just a pretext. Veronique looked genuinely stunned, as if she had not thought it possible that I could do that. She said nothing, just left the room and slammed the door.

In my script, there would have to be more. Perhaps dialogues that revealed the dramas of my dysfunctional family, the possible cause of my inability to maintain a relationship. In a conversation, I would tell Veronique what I'd half told her in real-life about my parents: how they didn't get along with each other, or so it seemed to me because each of them complained that the other didn't listen or even see.

"You look at me, but you don't see me, or what you see is a ghost," Mom would often say. Dad wouldn't ask her what she meant by that, at least not in my presence, so I never knew what that was about.

At some point as a teenager, I figured that Mom blamed him for not wanting to see her as she was then, but rather as she was when they were newlyweds, a kind of denial of the fact that she was aging, though she was still under fifty, and in my opinion had not changed much since I was little. Maybe it was something else, and the business with the ghost was a reference to another woman, a past affair. I might never untangle the meaning of that; it was no longer an issue I could address with them long distance, and I had no intention of returning to Colombia—not for the time being, and much less for that.

I looked sideways at the clock: it was ten o'clock. I thought of calling Elena to tell her I'd had a good time, or to say goodnight, or something else, just an excuse to hear her voice; I figured she would appreciate it. But just as I was about to do that, I changed my mind, I thought it would be too much. I was a little hyper with the scenes I'd imagined. Nothing had inspired me so far for a script until tonight.

The scene with Louise and her boyfriend in *Full Moon in Paris* came to my mind again for a few moments. Perhaps I could watch the movie before bed, I thought. I had it on DVD, it was included in a collection I'd bought a month ago. I looked at the shelf where I had my books and DVDs, and took the film out. I noticed that inside the cover there was a piece of paper folded in four with pictures of the posters of the original movie releases.

Looking at the images, I got a rush of memories of my high school senior year. Among other things, I remembered the day I saw the film at my neighborhood's cinema in Bogotá, at a festival of French cinema, when I felt my life had changed forever, and that come what may, one day I had to study film and make a movie. To my mind also came the unpleasant moment when I told Dad that I had no intention of becoming an executive at his company or marrying his lawyer's daughter—or some other woman—after doing a degree in industrial engineering, preferably in England as he had done, if I got a good scholarship, no loans. It had been five, almost six years since then, and I was still far from my goal of getting into a film program. Dad had reluctantly helped with my college tuition, but only if I did something practical; that's how I ended up with my Spanish teaching degree.

I started watching the film and let the plot take me away. Louise wants to spend the weekends in Paris, gets a small study in the city, gets lonely, talks on the phone, sees friends, goes to a party, has an affair with a musician. As I watched, I realized, first with curiosity, then with a little alarm, that Veronique looked a little like Louise: her posture, her way of talking, the unkempt hair, the dark circles under her eyes. I kept watching, looking for those similarities, but after a while the credits were rolling. I couldn't see the final scene in which Louise leaves the house where she lived with her boyfriend, and I wasn't in the mood to rewind the film.

FIVE

On the Friday of that week, the lawyers offered me a full-time job as a Spanish teacher and translator for six months, with an option to renew the contract for another six if we all agreed. The schedule would be flexible, provided it didn't affect our class times, which would increase from six to ten hours a week; the rest of the time would be for translating documents. I gladly accepted. The pay and conditions were excellent, better than I imagined. The first thing I thought was that my new life had begun once and for all; from that point forward, all would be well, and I could already start making plans for the future, something that had seemed impossible to me only a week ago.

Elena didn't answer when I called to tell her the news, so I texted it, also confirming that I would pick her up in the evening. We had arranged to meet at seven to go to Lisa's place; she'd invited the group for dinner. I had not seen Elena since the day we went to the Nikko to look for the samurai. That night, she got a cold that turned into the flu, and kept her in bed for the rest of the week.

All these evenings we chatted on the phone about anything, sometimes for more than an hour, with the effortless ease of old friends. Whatever it was we talked about, though, our conversations invariably led to her mom. It was clear that their relationship was very important, but they apparently quarreled very often, especially recently, because Elena went back to insisting that she tell her more about her father, an issue that the two had agreed to leave aside. When Elena mentioned something related to it, I kept quiet and let her blow off some steam; I didn't tell her what I thought, only that I understood. Sometimes what I really thought and wanted to say was I really understood her mother, and it was already high time to put the ghosts of the past behind. As for me, I hardly ever mentioned my family, I couldn't think of anything resembling the issues with her mom, or any other reason. The only person I talked to at home was mom, and we never argued.

I was walking down Market Street—the lawyers' office was near Embarcadero, a few blocks back—and was about to turn on Grant as if going to the Ansonia, as if I were still living there; I'd done this many times in the past, though in a very different state of mind. I stopped in my tracks and blurted out a laugh; in my excitement, I had forgotten to make a turn on the street where I always took the bus on my way home. At that moment, a cable car's bell rang, announcing its departure. It had a red cab with advertisements for an art museum on the sides, and it was full of people, some standing on the running board, hanging on to the side poles. I looked absently at the scene and remembered that I had been there with Mom and Dad about six years ago in September, when I first came to the city, having recently settled in Berkeley in an apartment I shared with other students.

I had buried that memory, or perhaps it had gotten entangled with others of the many times that I'd walked around there, downcast and unemployed, as I told Elena one night. I remembered that on that first visit I had been very impressed with the city, which until then I only knew through movies and TV shows. Mom and Dad also loved it; they walked everywhere and took tons of pictures. It was their first time on the West Coast, and the next day they went back to Colombia. It was the last time I'd seen them.

The day was overcast and gray, but I felt happy and full of energy. What a difference it made to have a good job and to be starting a relationship that looked promising.

Since I was downtown I decided to do some

shopping; I needed shoes, maybe a shirt, and definitely some books that would help me with work. As I crossed Union Square, looking at the palm trees on the way to the department store, I had the feeling it was the first time I was there, or rather that I *saw* myself there, although I'd walked through the area many times and had spent quite a bit of time sitting on one of the benches people watching or listening to street musicians.

After shopping, I made my way to the Argosy bookstore on Sutter Street. With a cool head now, I felt a shade of concern because part of my job would be translating some Portuguese documents, and I had not read in that language for a long while, more than a year now. I thought maybe a novel or two would help me catch up.

The lawyers took me by surprise with that bit; they mentioned it last, as an add-on. We were ready to pack up when Miryam, the youngest of the partners, said that it was a pleasant surprise that my college degree was in Romance languages, Spanish and Portuguese, because she had a pending case, a property lawsuit, and there were some Portuguese documents that needed translation. The other two partners looked at each other and then at me, and almost by reflex I said yes, no problem.

The bookstore was almost empty at that hour, just a middle-aged couple browsing old maps, in the mezzanine. I got distracted in the film section; some of the books were on sale for half price. They had a good assortment of titles on European directors; some of the books they had in the university library, which I had read in bits and pieces. One of the books on sale about the history of Japanese cinema caught my attention; it had a fancy cover, like a collage of posters. It was the cheapest book, just five dollars, so I decided to buy it; I thought that it would somehow bring me closer to Elena.

I asked one of the booksellers, a rotund, balding man who spoke with a British accent, if they had literature in Portuguese. He said maybe one or two titles, and that they had stopped buying foreign language books. Customers didn't show much interest, and it was difficult to compete with online bookstores. We went to the foreign language section, and on the Portuguese shelves found a bilingual edition of sonnets by Luís de Camões and a novella by Antonio Tabucchi—an author I didn't know—titled *Noturno Indiano*, which turned out to be translated from the Italian. The two books were also on sale; in total I spent a little over fifteen dollars.

Elena greeted me warmly with a big hug and took me by the hand to her room. She had just showered, and her hair still damp; not as bluish as before, it was now darker, more its natural color. She still looked a bit unwell, her eyes a little red as if she'd been crying.

I had another big argument with Mom today, she said while she picked up some charcoal sketches of birds and fish lying on the ground, perhaps studies for an oil painting. It was unpleasant, you know, but she told me more about my father.

What about him?

That he had many debts, and the films he worked on were apparently B-grade; some were not even distributed.

I don't know what you mean by B-grade, I said.

Mom is not very straightforward, and to make matters worse, she doesn't speak English well, nor do I speak Spanish well. I don't know how we managed all these years. Anyway, she said that after my father left for good, she learned through some of the other Japanese customers who went to the restaurant where she worked, that he had a bad reputation, and his projects were usually trashy, and that he owed money to everyone, even to the *yakuza* mafia. By then, my father was hardly around. According to Mom, he spent only about a week out of every month with us; the rest of the time he was traveling, mostly in Singapore and Japan, supposedly working.

What do you mean trashy? I asked. We always spoke English, but she said that word in Spanish.

That was the word she used. But for her, many things are trashy. She says it so often that it is not clear what she means exactly. I asked her to explain it, but she got it all mixed up; or perhaps I couldn't make sense of it, and she got furious, said it wasn't worth it, and hung up on me.

Trashy could mean that it wasn't worth much, I said.

Elena frowned and then burst out laughing. You're right; I mean, I think that's what she meant, that the films weren't worthwhile, that they lacked quality. But that doesn't make it clearer. It's a subjective judgment, right?

Perhaps she watched some of his films, I ventured.

I doubt it. Mom doesn't like movies, and she barely watches TV. None of that interests her. What she likes are *trashy* romance novels; she's always reading one. You see what happens? I'm now talking like her.

Do you know his name?

His name is or was Hiroki Ibuke, but according to Mom, he sometimes used other names.

I wanted to ask if she had tried to find him under his own name, but I held back. I thought it was better to try to change the topic, to move away from the idea of her father, which was turning into an obsession.

At about seven we took a taxi to Lisa's house in North Beach. The evening was pleasant: a clear sky, a hint of chill, and not much wind. On the way, Elena didn't say anything; she looked out the window the entire time, a little withdrawn, perhaps still thinking about her father.

We were the last to arrive. We found our friends nursing aperitifs, already seated at the table. The house looked different than the week before. Veronique had put some of her things in the living room, some pieces of Mexican pottery that we had bought together at an art fair on the fireplace, pieces of Thai silk in bright colors draping the sofa, and some French novels on the shelves. On the dining room wall, I saw a framed picture I had not seen the other night, a group shot of us in black and white that Felipe took on a sunny afternoon in Fort Point, overlooking Golden Gate Bridge, perhaps a gift he made for Veronique and Lisa for the occasion.

Another reason to toast, Lisa said as we sat down.

The table was set formally, with several glasses for wine and water and all kinds of cutlery. A line of lit candlesticks went from one side to the table to the other.

Did we miss something? Elena asked.

Nothing you didn't already know, dear, Veronique

said, and took Lisa's hand, who was sitting next to her. I say that because of you two. Cheers.

After toasting, Veronique went to the kitchen and served the meal: vegetable soup first, then a chicken stew with potatoes and vegetables. Lisa dimmed the lights until we were in semidarkness, something that reminded me of our gatherings at the Ansonia.

During the meal, we talked about our plans for the future. It was a sort of tradition in the group that had begun when we started going out together and most of us were unemployed, as a way of talking about the kind of future we would like.

Our future could be in Korea, Lisa said.

The two of us could work teaching languages over there, Veronique added, clearing her throat. The Alliance Française in Seoul usually has openings throughout the year; it's not like here, where there are so many French people and so few classes. Moreover, the visa is easier to get; it's not as complicated as in this country.

Not so fast, please, Felipe said, raising his hands and looking from side to side as if he had misheard and was looking for an explanation from the rest of us.

Tell us again, please, Lydia added, who also looked surprised, her face slightly flushed—something that often happened when she was upset. There is so much news today. I'm not sure I can digest all of this at once.

Is it an idea, or is it a plan?

An idea, for the time being, Lisa said. Maybe for next semester—my contract at school is flexible—I could take a leave of absence.

Ricardo and I met some recruiters from a Japanese language school with branches in Korea, Elena said. I have a brochure with contact information; I could lend it to you, if you'd like, Elena said, looking at Lisa. I am also thinking of something along those lines, she added in a lower tone, dragging out the words as if it had just occurred to her and she was considering it for the first time.

I felt somewhat uncomfortable when I heard that. It didn't surprise me that Elena said it; it was inevitable that she was thinking of going to Japan to search for her father. I said nothing, but I felt everyone was now looking at me. What could I say? My affair with Elena was just beginning. We would have to be together for a while longer for me to be affected by Elena's ideas or plans.

I'm interested in the business with the Alliance Française in Korea, Lydia said suddenly, and all eyes turned to her. How do you know about the openings? Do they advertise anywhere?

In language-teaching websites mostly, Lisa said. There are all kinds of openings, including for Spanish. No experience needed.

You and Ricardo could teach Spanish, Lydia said to Felipe with a wink.

Veronique burst out laughing, and we all stared at her for an instant, and then everyone laughed.

The beauty of this scenario, Lisa said, is that it's perfectly possible. We could talk about it seriously, if you're interested.

Well, it's not an option for me, Felipe said. I need to get residency in the United States. Korea is far away. Besides, teaching is not for me. I tried that in Guadalajara at the university, and I was lousy at it.

You don't have to be a real teacher in Korea, Lisa said. Just speak the language well.

I'm not sure I would go to Korea; but to Japan, I would go, Elena said. Isn't it pretty much the same, Lisa?

I think that the salaries are better, though not by much, Lisa replied. But I understand they require more qualifications.

The recruiters we met said they were flexible with qualifications, Elena said. She now looked animated; her cheeks had more color than before.

It's all the same to me, Lydia said. Japan, Korea, China—what's the difference? They are all far from France, and that's the way I like it.

Same for me, Lisa said. In fact, I think it would be a better idea to go to Japan; I've heard you work less over there and earn more.

I looked from one end to the table to the other, and I felt that in the end it would be my friends who would pull away from me, not the other way around. Only Felipe and I had planned a future in this country. They could go away anytime they wanted. Although, now that I thought about it, Felipe could also go; he didn't have anything that would tie him up here. My situation was different, I had a chance to stay permanently: Mom was a citizen, having been born in New York, and thanks to that, I was applying for US citizenship.

I looked again at my friends one by one; they were all engrossed in conversations about whether it was a good plan to go to Japan or Korea. Elena looked at me sideways; she was talking with Lisa, perhaps about the ins and outs of teaching English, what books to use or something like that. Lydia also listened attentively. Veronique suddenly started collecting the dishes; she looked focused on her domestic work, like an old-fashioned housewife. That's what came to my mind.

I laughed to myself because it was not the first time I saw my friends getting excited about an idea or a scenario in which we would all be together; sometimes it was a business venture where we could all be partners, or a trip or adventure we would undertake. I felt a little sad because the scenario they were contemplating in the Far East was not for me.

SIX

Javier Pinto wrote back, said Elena without a shadow of surprise in her voice. We had just finished eating and were sitting in her living room, Elena with her laptop, as usual. I knew Elena had written to Pinto last week, after the gathering at Lisa's, but I hadn't asked what she'd said; I didn't want to know the particulars at that time.

What does he tell you? I asked.

He wrote a long email, with lots of information. Shall I read it to you?

Better give me a summary, I replied. I felt uncomfortable and a bit annoyed; the idea of listening to what would be Pinto's voice telling Elena about a job she'd like that would take her to Japan in the near future did not appeal to me. Besides I was tired, still not used to working all day.

Elena nodded and looked at her computer. He says I would have to do the paperwork through the Japanese consulate, which takes several weeks, but that it would be easy if everything was in order. He also says that my MFA in studio arts would be an advantage—they would pay me a little more, and in the future, if I wanted to stay and could speak Japanese, I could use it to teach art at a university.

You could already teach art at a university here, I said.

I could, but I don't want to; I'm not interested at the moment, and I don't know if I would be good at it.

You might be good at it. It's a matter of giving it a shot, I replied.

Elena looked at me and raised her eyebrows for a moment. Perhaps I sounded angry, and she was taken aback.

The salary they offer is better than I what I make at the hotel, Elena added, her eyes back on the computer screen. Health insurance is very cheap, plus they pay for transportation.

While Elena said this, I looked away toward the wall, where once hung the painting of the hurricane or whirlwind that blended with the half light of the room. Now there was nothing in its place, but I could still see the hole it had left, or rather I *felt* it; the shadows around it seemed sharper.

Look, Pinto also says that with your teaching certificate they would pay you a bit more.

Did you tell him I was interested?

I mentioned it as a possibility.

But you know I'm not interested, I said.

Well, whatever you want, Ricardo. I'll answer Javier tomorrow, but I have to think what to write. I don't want to commit to anything; I've seen other jobs like that online with similar pay packages. Let's change the subject. How are your lawyers?

I don't know why, but it occurred to me that Elena had been talking to Veronique about me. Elena was not the type to delay or postpone discussing something important; that was Veronique's style: more cautious, though it didn't always pay off. I knew that since the last time we met at Lisa's, the two spoke every day, and they seemed closer than before. Perhaps they talked about the best way to convince me to join their plan to go to Japan. Veronique had also written to Javier Pinto with several questions, and I assumed he would have already answered.

Things are going very well, I replied. I'd never imagined that what lawyers do could be so interesting.

Would you like to become a lawyer?

I've never really thought about it. When I was little, I had a bad impression of lawyers. I always heard my dad say they were scoundrels you couldn't trust. I don't believe that now, of course.

You see? Things are never what they seem, she said, and she looked at me with a half smile.

I see things more closely now, although I don't always understand how they work. Sometimes I have the impression that our firm is one of those nonprofit organizations that advocate for human rights and things like that.

And that surprises you?

A little. Miryam, the youngest, is working on a property lawsuit in Macau, in China, which at bottom is a human rights case, something related to World War Two and the Japanese army.

That sounds complicated, Elena said.

It also has to do with human trafficking and other illegal stuff.

You say Miryam is the youngest. How old is she?

Forty? I don't know. I don't pay much attention to that.

Of course not, honey. You're blind as a bat, Elena said, and burst out laughing.

The human trafficking bit is horrible; it makes me think of my cousin who vanished, I said, a bit annoyed. It bothered me that Elena sometimes focused on petty details; it gave me the impression that it was all she cared about with my new job.

Have you heard anything about her? Elena asked,

and closed her laptop.

I asked my mother a few days ago, but she said she didn't know anything for certain: Sofía, who is Adriana's mother, recently learned that she lived in another city, in Yokohama, apparently, and that she had a new job, but nothing else.

As a nurse?

Now, I doubt that it's nursing, I said, and suddenly and despite myself I remembered my old desire for Adriana, something that had been lying dormant in a corner of my consciousness for a long time, perhaps since I left Colombia. It was an awkward sensation I couldn't make sense of at the time and had to make an effort to make it fade away immediately. I hate to say it, but I think my dad was right, I went on, still uncomfortable, perhaps feeling guilty, and aware that it was a topic that was best left aside (after all, Elena didn't need to know about it). Perhaps she's doing something else, I added. I understand there are some Colombian women who go to Japan to work as escorts, and things like that. Adriana studied nursing, but she has an associate degree, which is lower than a registered nurse degree. My mom explained this to me the other day, and I don't see how it could have been enough to get a work visa in Japan, even for a nursing home. You know how difficult it is for language teachers.

You sound like an expert now. You weren't that interested before, Elena said and sat next to me on the sofa.

I've been translating from the Spanish a report from a nonprofit organization in Mexico that works on these issues in Europe and Asia, I said. I was very surprised by the statistics: there are many women from several countries in Latin America, and from Mexico as well.

They all go to Japan?

To Singapore, Macau, Hong Kong, and Seoul, also, I replied.

All this in your first week, Elena said and left the phrase in the air. Let's go out back, she added. I have a bottle of wine that would do us good.

Great idea, I said. That weekend I would again stay with Elena, and I wanted to forget all about work, have a few drinks, sleep late. The routine at work had taken its toll on me. Although in theory I didn't have to worry about getting up at the same time every day, all week I had gotten up around seven and arrived at the office early, before the lawyers, who started to come at around nine o'clock. Elena and I had decided that we would see each other on weekends; it would be very difficult for us to figure out a schedule to meet during the week; she still had her evening shifts at the Ansonia, slept late in the mornings, and did her artwork in the afternoons.

Elena uncorked the bottle and poured us drinks. That evening the view from the terrace was spectacular. The sun had fallen, but the sky still had a purple glow with patches of orange toward the horizon. From afar came an echo of music, perhaps from Castro Street, where there was a fair this weekend with live performances.

I'll tell you my mom's story, Elena said after a short while. It's time I tell you the whole story so you understand where I'm at now. Elena's tone was serious, in her face a shadow of concern, as if whatever she was about to say would be a revelation that would change everything. I figured she'd been thinking about this for several days.

Like me, my mom grew up without a father, she said. Well, she had a father for ten years, and then he died of stomach cancer. My grandfather didn't leave much money. I think he was a real piece of work; he apparently had several lovers and money troubles. Faced with the looming financial situation, my grandmother took Mom out of the private school she was attending, and put her to work in a grocery store or something like that; we are talking about the 1960s in Mexico, and there were no strict laws against that. When my mom turned eighteen, she decided to run away. She didn't want to go on living with my grandmother because they didn't get along. According to Mom, she was exploiting her, and all the money she earned went to her expenses; she was used to certain luxuries with my grandfather: dining out, going dancing, buying new clothes. Mom's plan was to come to the United States no matter what. I think she'd had this idea since she was little—don't ask me why. That's the way my mom is. When she gets something into her head, no one can convince her otherwise. Mom went to live with her best friend from school in a small apartment in Coyoacán, a suburb of Mexico City. This friend was studying acting at the National Institute of Fine Arts, and through her, my mom met an actor called Pedro Armendáriz. Apparently they got along very well—just friends nothing more—and after a few months, Armendáriz told her that if she wanted to come to the United States, he would help her cross the border; in those days it was not so difficult.

Is this Pedro Armendáriz the father or son? I asked. The two made films in Hollywood—James Bond movies also.

She met the two, but it was the son who helped her. What a great cinema memory you have. You should do something with it. Tell me later why you haven't. In any case, that's how my mom came to the United States.

When she made it to Los Angeles, Armendáriz got her a job at a Mexican restaurant where many film people, including some Hollywood stars, went. That's where she met my father. I told you all of that.

Elena stopped her story, and served us a round of drinks. It was now completely dark, a clear moonless sky with some scattered stars, small bright dots in the sky.

What I've told you is pretty much what my mom has always told me, give or take a few details, Elena said after we toasted. But yesterday she told me something that left me puzzled. We were talking about Armendáriz because he's now better known in the United States. This month he's in a Richard Rodriguez film; I don't know if you've read about it, but it's a film in the style of Sergio Leone, the Italian who made westerns—spaghetti westerns, they were called. My mom read a note about it in a Spanish newspaper in Los Angeles; since we were on the subject of newspapers, we went on to talk about my father's picture, the one in the newspaper clipping she's kept all these years, where he appears with other Japanese men. I reminded Mom that I'm waiting for her to send it to me. When I get it, I'll scan it and run it through Photoshop to see if I can get a better look at his face, though I doubt it, because the paper is very old, and the ink must have faded. Anyway, we were talking about the clipping when she said it was a pity that the other picture got ruined, because my father looked better in it. I asked her what picture, and Mom laughed; she asked me, *Don't you remember?* and then said: *Of course, mija, how can you remember? You were so little.* I got angry with Mom then: it's so typical of her saying things like that in passing, and so casually, as if they were not important.

They are important to *you*, I said. Your mom wants to leave that aside.

For her it would have been better if it hadn't happened, Elena replied, pinching me lightly on my arm.

The fact is, there was another photo, Elena went on. Mom said it was of my father in a mariachi suit. It seems it was one of those promotional photos that actors take for their CVs—or whatever you call what they use to apply for jobs—and she had it framed, and placed it on her dressing table with other personal effects: the little costume jewelry she wore, a container with perfume, stuff like that. According to her, I didn't like the picture. Sometimes I cried when I looked at it, although it was not clear if it was perhaps something else; on the table there was also a cross and an image of the Virgin of Guadalupe. I was very resistant when it came to religion; luckily, she never insisted. Mom told me that one day when she was not looking, I started playing with the stuff on her dressing table and accidentally dropped a glass of orange juice on the picture, and so it got ruined. She said she got so angry with me that she slapped me on the face, and from that day forward I didn't touch her things again. For Mom that's the important part of the story: discipline because it was my fault; the fact that it was a picture of my father falls to the background. Anyway, that's how my mom is.

Do you think the photo was from a movie? I asked. Isn't it odd to see a Japanese man in a mariachi suit?

Mom says that my father said it was a still frame from a movie, but she didn't believe him and thought it was a joke. Why would a Japanese act in a film as a mariachi? There you have another example of how my mom thinks. If she thinks something is not possible, it is not.

Do you know if there is a Japanese film about mariachis, or at least about Mexico? I asked.

I looked it up on the Net, but couldn't find anything, or rather, nothing relevant.

Anyway, it's a good clue, I said. You'd have to ask an expert, perhaps a university professor.

I'm on it. I already found a couple in California, both of Mexican background, by the way. I'll keep you posted.

You know why I tell you all this, Ricardo?

Tell me.

Because I've always felt that I am not who I *should* be, that I'm missing a piece in the puzzle of my life, and that it has to do with my father. I don't know if you understand what I mean.

I understand that you need to know who your father is. But, I also suspect that it's not necessarily what you need to know.

What do you mean?

You are your own person, and the essence of who you are is inside, not outside.

It could be. But my intuition tells me that getting to know my father will be the key that will lead me inside.

Elena served us another drink and leaned back in her chair. I did the same and stretched my legs and arms. I felt very much at ease with Elena next to me, and I looked forward to another night together. The echo of music continued; an electric-bass sound wafted through in waves, and it added to the faint roar of traffic. Friday nights in the Castro district were always lively. After a few minutes, Elena was dozing. It was odd for her to fall asleep so early; it was I, with my new routine, who should be yawning by now. I thought maybe the wine had made her sleepy. I noticed a thin dark line coming down from the corner of her right eye, perhaps a painted line; it was unusual because Elena wore very little makeup. Or maybe it was the trace of a tear.

SEVEN

One morning a few weeks later, Veronique called to invite me to lunch; she said she had something important to tell me—nothing urgent, but she'd rather do it in person. I said I could spare no more than a half hour and it would have to be in a restaurant near the office. I was very busy these days; apart from my normal workload, I was serving as an interpreter for some foreign guests, members of a nonprofit organization in Mexico with whom the lawyers had agreed to work as a team with other lawyers in Washington and Hong Kong.

We met at Embarcadero Plaza, and from there went to a Mexican *taqueria* that had recently opened south of Market, near the bus station. The sky was getting cloudy, and on the street ran a whistling wind that lifted up dust and loose debris.

Lisa and I decided to go to Tokyo, Veronique said when we were about to start eating. Pinto has been very efficient with our applications; he's already mailed us our contracts. We'll teach in the same school, and the pay is good; Lisa will make more, of course. The place was a bit noisy, but I could hear Veronique fine. Our table was at the back, where there were not many customers, in a small room decorated with a mural of a mariachi group playing in a Mexican town square painted in bright colors.

This is good news, I said. When are you traveling?

That's what I wanted to talk to you about, Veronique said. The next teaching cycle starts in late February, which is in three months, and we've already applied for a visa.

And what you'd like to know is whether I've given further thought to the plan?

Elena says you don't want to talk about it. She doesn't understand why. What's going on? I'm not here on her behalf; don't even think about it. I would never do that. But you know that I love you both, and it would hurt me if you drift apart from each other. I think you make a perfect couple. I always figured that, you know? Call it intuition or whatever you want.

I felt a little angry at Veronique's words, not so much because of what she said, but because of the matter-of-fact way she said it; it reminded me of our days together, which were now fading away from my memory.

One thing at a time, Veronique, I said. First of all,

my relationship with Elena is fine, thank you. And, I'll be grateful if you don't stick your nose into our business.

You don't sound like yourself, Ricardo, Veronique said in a calm and mechanical tone. Since you left the Ansonia, you've changed a lot. Don't think I'm the only one who's noticed it.

For some reason Veronique's words made me feel that we'd already had this conversation when we were dating, a kind of déjà vu: Veronique poked her nose in my business, I told her off, she told me I was not myself. I tried to remember what came next, but the feeling faded, and I was back in real time. Veronique looked at me somewhat impatiently.

Sorry, I said. The whole thing worries me, of course, you can't imagine how much; but right now, I can't afford to play with my life. I don't know how to explain it better. I have to decide what it is I want to do in the future. If I go to Japan, it'll be like postponing that decision, you know? Besides, I'm not interested in Japan. Yes, I'm curious, but it's the same curiosity I feel for Tibet or Bhutan. It's not enough to change my life at this point.

And your relationship with Elena? Don't you think that's more important? What if she turns out to be the love of your life?

I'd rather not talk about it now, Veronique. Let's leave that aside, shall we? I'll talk to Elena soon, and you'll hear about it in due course.

Veronique looked at me with a shadow of concern. Maybe she was now taking me seriously. I didn't regret what I'd said, but I was surprised I'd said it. For the past few days, I'd been thinking about talking to Elena about her plans for the future and of our relationship, but I hadn't felt like it or had the courage to do it; she also hadn't taken the initiative. It was as if we had both agreed postponing something that was inevitable—perhaps our breakup. Veronique was still watching me, frowning slightly, probably with disapproval or reproach. But I couldn't tell her anything more at the moment. Certainly not that I was very much in love, and that like her, I would do anything to be with Elena—if she was the love of my life, I didn't know yet. Our relationship was just beginning; it had to evolve naturally.

OK, let's leave that aside for now, Veronique said suddenly, putting her hands on the table. I hope you find the right words to tell Elena whatever it is you decide.

You talk a lot with her, I said and left the phrase up in the air. From the street came the sound of a distant rattle; I could make out through the window in the main room that it was suddenly raining copiously. Some passersby entered the main room in a rush to shelter from the rain; they were already soaked. Also surprised, Veronique turned to look for a moment.

No more than usual, Veronique replied, and stared at me, her brow still furrowed. We've always talked a lot, and often. Maybe you hadn't noticed...

I interrupted. I want to take things one at a time. I didn't want to hear any more complaints about how much I'd changed or anything like that. I don't want to make drastic decisions, I said in a lower tone; I thought I had been a little loud before. I've already told you how hard it was to become independent, all the drama with my family, and the loans I had to take. You'll understand I don't want to take any steps backward. I think this job with the law firm will help me out a lot; perhaps it's the beginning of a career. It is an important opportunity in my life; I don't want to waste it. I thought—but didn't say it—that I wasn't as lucky as she was with a wealthy family, not to mention the advantages of French citizenship; I'd told her that once, perhaps upset with a comment she might have made about my fears of being aimless and unemployed.

Veronique finished eating and now listened to me with one hand on her chin, a typical gesture of hers when she concentrated. Unwittingly, or perhaps because part of my mind was digging into the past, I remembered a night with her at the Ansonia, one of the first we spent together: we barely slept, we spent the time talking and making love in my room, which was large and dim as a cave, because one of the lamps wasn't working.

At some point, she stretched out on the bed, listening to what I was saying, chin in hand, dark circles around her eyes, her tangled hair, dark and shiny, strewn across her back. I was telling her about my holiday trips when I was little; we had talked about hers; she'd traveled a lot. She was an only child, and her parents took her backpacking everywhere in Europe and Asia; they were like hippies. I told her that in Colombia, we always traveled by road; my dad loved to drive; he used to say it was his hobby. For Easter we went to visit my grandparents on Mom's side to a town about three hours from Bogotá; for the end-of-the-year holidays, to the Caribbean, a long two-day trip up and down mountains, from the cold highlands to the steaming lowlands, passing through many towns and some cities, sometimes stopping at the side of the road to watch the valleys and rivers or eat local delicacies, cheeses and fresh fruit, or enjoy the smell of the dry or humid countryside, depending on where we were.

Veronique liked it when I gave many details; she used to ask me many questions, wanted to know everything. Perhaps it helped her to write. That night she'd asked me about my grandparents; she was intrigued by my dad's prejudice against them for being from the countryside, or for being poor, or both, and my answers had sparked many memories, some random, buried very deep in my mind. When I told her about my grandparents that night, I spoke of things I'd almost forgotten—for example, of some picture frames and jewelry boxes in their narrow living room that had an exquisite marquetry, inlaid with bone and tortoiseshell that Dad called *baroque*—a word he said with disdain. He preferred modern styles; he didn't like antiques. One of the frames had a photograph of my great-grandfather that I always looked closely at: he was a tall, swarthy, handsome man who looked like Mom in the eyes and mouth. I also told her about the house's backyard, larger than the house itself, which had several fruit trees: one a papaya, another one a mango; I remembered the aroma of the ripe fruits and the jellies and sweets my grandmother made with them. Sulfur vapors sometimes came in bursts from the hot springs by the river; Dad hated the smell, always complained about it, though we rarely went to my grandparents; usually they came to visit us. We stayed at the best hotel in town on the main square; Dad liked luxury, plus he'd get bored with my grandparents because they lacked refinement, he said, and had nothing to talk about.

A feeling of nostalgia came over me for the fullness of life I'd felt before, something that had escaped me for a long while, though now that I thought about it, I'd felt something like that during those early days with Veronique; it was a shame that our relationship didn't work out. To my mind came again Veronique lying in bed, chin in hand, dark circles around her eyes, her tangled hair dark and shiny strewn across her back.

There was a flash of lightning, and after one, two, three, four seconds, a loud roar of thunder; the lightning had struck far away. The entire restaurant fell into momentary silence; the other patrons, equally surprised, stopped talking. After a few seconds, the clatter of rain relented as the storm moved on.

Miryam, the youngest of the lawyers, was standing by the doorway; she was one of the passersby caught by the rain who'd come in a few minutes ago. She was wearing a trench coat with the collar up, like the samurai, a small mangled umbrella in hand, very likely prey of the gusty winds. Our eyes met, and she smiled and told me, just mouthed, that she was soaked. Her loose dark hair was dripping; the umbrella had done little for her. I waved at her to come to our table, but she shook her head, and with her finger pointing at her watch mouthed that she was late and had to run, and after a moment she did. Two other people left after her, probably also late for their meetings.

It was my boss, I told Veronique, who had witnessed our last exchange—she'd turned around when I was waving at Miryam. She probably just arrived by bus to the station across the street, I added. She lives in a town across the bay, beyond Oakland, and has no car; she says she's not interested in driving.

Your lawyer looks Asian, Veronique said, looking puzzled. Where's she from?

You sound like Elena, who's taken an interest in my bosses, I said. I don't ask them anything personal, and they don't ask me either. I know she's Dutch, but her mother was Chinese, if I'm not mistaken. At work, they only talk about the law; they are very professional, too serious, if you'd like to know. Which reminds me that I have many things to do, I added, and put my cell phone and keys in my pocket, getting ready to leave. To my mind came my little office—its large windows overlooking the Embarcadero's three buildings and the sea beyond—and several folders on my desk of work to do. I have to go, I told Veronique, but I promise I'll think things through. Don't think I don't care about what you told me.

Okay, she replied and gave me a big hug when we got up. I'll call you later. Don't go away from me.

That afternoon I couldn't concentrate at work. I was translating into Spanish a report from the State Department on human trafficking for our Mexican guests. The report was concise, very straightforward, and easy to understand in English. It was about recent legislation, and it invoked international law, but I found myself unsure of what words to use in Spanish, I couldn't think of the right terms, though I was familiar with legal terminology. I'd done translations in the other direction; perhaps my mind was not up to it. There was a whole section on the concept of compelled service and modern slavery that was quite confusing; I would have to ask Miryam, who knew these laws better than anyone and always gave me long-winded explanations, as if I were in law school.

I paused and looked out the window; it was still raining, the raindrops falling in thick uniform and transparent threads to the street ten stories below. The scene seemed unreal; I could not hear the rain, and there was a hollow silence, because the windows were very thick with insulation. I've always liked the murmur of the rain. As a child, I was fascinated to see rain. My bedroom windows and those in the living room overlooked Bogota's eastern mountains, hefty and green with patches of dense forest, the rain clouds like feathery swaths of gauze changing forms over them. When these images come to mind, they also bring the pleasant feeling of breathing fresh air after rain, I always opened the windows and took deep breaths; it was something that came to me almost instinctively.

I thought about that night with Veronique at the Ansonia and the triggered memories that flooded back again, especially now, watching the rain. Once again I remembered Veronique lying in bed, her tangled hair, dark and shiny, strewn across her back. What made me remember that night? Was it the intensity of that moment? Perhaps it was that, because these days *I did not feel it.* It did not come to me; it didn't happen with Elena; I could not reach that *intensity.* Another memory came into my mind through that open window to the mountains: it was a song my mom often played when she was feeling nostalgic or sad, and also when she watched the rain—sometimes it was the both of us looking at it—Pablo Milanés sang it, a sad song, also cryptic, which in the beginning went: *Many times I've told you that before we did it, we had to think it through, that this togetherness of us needed more of our bodies and desire also*, a line that I always thought was tragic, about a failed or wilted relationship. Perhaps that was what happened to Mom and Dad's relationship; perhaps that was the secret or the ghost that Mom alluded to when she'd reproachfully tell my dad that he didn't see her. I had the song on my cell phone;

I listened to it from time to time, though not recently, and right now, this instant, it seemed to me linked to the present. I thought I'd listen to it even if only for a minute, but no sooner had I touched the phone than I decided to put it off until later; I thought I would listen to it on my way home under the rain, when I would have more time.

I repeated the lyrics in my mind, and unwittingly Elena's face came to me as a corresponding image, like the visual representation of the words. I thought of the lyrics without the music in an imaginary conversation with Elena as an explanation of why it was not a good idea to stick together, and I thought it fit well; or rather I felt that it wouldn't not go well. Perhaps it was true, and we *needed more of our bodies and desire also.* With Veronique it had been quite different: she was very passionate, very given to the moment, very aware of what she wanted to feel and make you feel.

With Elena, when we make love, I sometimes have the impression that she's not there, or only partially there, as if just passing by. If I had to compare, I would also say that I felt more passion for Veronique than I feel for Elena now. Elena and I understand each other better, and this is an advantage; we also anticipate each other's reactions and moods, making our relationship more stable and predictable, something that bodes well for the future, if we think long term.

But this was a sensitive issue; I had to think it through and then discuss it with Elena, better sooner than later. I would not see her for two days, until the weekend. What would I say to her? I suddenly felt a twinge in my stomach, a kind of uneasiness; or was it a certainty that this would be our last conversation as a couple? Through the window the rain continued to fall, uniform and silent, the clouds like feathery swaths of gauze changing forms.

EIGHT

I have something important to tell you about my father, Elena said when we left the gallery. Let's go to the bar around the corner where we used to go to listen to jazz, OK?

I gladly accepted. I'd been a little bored at the show's opening where some of the artists gave speeches about art and human rights that ran longer than necessary, with side political commentary and talk about the upcoming presidential elections. Elena had a good time chatting with some of them; I interpreted whenever necessary—luckily, it wasn't about legal matters.

It was cold and windy out on the street, and it had been like that all week; the news said it was unusual to have such winter weather, as if we were already in January.

We sat at the bar and ordered two beers.

Remember I told you I was going to write to some professors about Japanese movies filmed in Mexico? Elena asked.

I nodded slightly, though at first I didn't know what she was talking about—I didn't remember having discussed movies with Elena recently; her mentioning professors reminded me it had to do with her father's movies. I'd had a chaotic day at the office editing translations of documents from one language to the other, and my head was spinning morning and afternoon; at one point with a mild panic I realized that I could no longer remember which were the originals and which the translations.

Well, one of them replied, Elena went on, a Chicano named Gómez at UC Santa Cruz, said he knew of at least one, but he had not watched it, because apparently it was not distributed internationally. The title is something like *Adventures in Mexico.* According to Gómez it's a Western. What would you call that? *¿Sushi Western?* Elena shrugged and looked at me, as if I had the answer to that.

I had no idea that the Japanese did Westerns, I said.

Me neither, Elena said, and sipped her beer. Gómez doesn't know much about the film other than what's on the net, which is not much. It sounds like a story about honor. The protagonist travels to Mexico in search of his best friend, who has been unjustly accused of a crime, but can't find him because he's become a bandit with a heart of gold: a sort of Robin Hood, who steals from the rich to give to the poor. Luckily, there was also a poster, she added.

Did you see the poster?

Yes, I saw it. You wouldn't believe how shocked I was. It took my breath away. I kid you not! I sent you an SMS text right away, but you didn't reply.

I was working, but I called you a little while after; don't you remember?

Yeah, yeah, sorry, I forgot. I was telling Lisa and Veronique on the landline. Anyway, when I saw the poster, I suddenly remembered the picture that my mom had on her night table. The photo I ruined with orange juice! It was, *is*, the same picture: a Japanese man dressed in *charro* costume—I mean, my *father*. I recognized him immediately, I was dead certain. Don't ask me how.

Did you talk to your mom?

Yes of course. I sent the picture to her cell, and she confirmed that it was him. She was very surprised. In fact, she shouted, *Virgen santísima*, *Blessed Virgin, it's a ghost*, and when she came to herself, she again told me what she's always told me, that I should leave that aside, that I shouldn't look for this man who was not worth it, who was not my father in the legal sense of the word, much less my *real* father. But as I've told you before, I need to know him now more than ever. I'm pretty sure it's the man we saw in North Beach that night.

Pretty sure?

Yeah, let me show you the picture, and you'll see what I mean, she said, and turned on her cell phone.

The man in the poster had Asian features, was in his early thirties, had tanned skin, and a thin mustache. He was dressed in a white embroidered shirt and black pants with side stripes, definitely a *charro* cowboy costume, on his head a large wide-brimmed hat.

OK, I see the resemblance, but it doesn't convince me, I said. It could be any Japanese man.

Look at the pose, Elena said, pointing with her extended index finger at the image. Remember that?

The man on the poster was playing the bandit: he had a gun in his right hand, pointing slightly upward, the trigger raised as a thumb, the barrel as an extended index finger. It was an aggressive pose, though it also had irony or clumsiness; the gesture on his face baring his teeth wasn't convincing—more posing than real anger. Perhaps he wasn't a good actor.

It's possible, I said. It could be the samurai.

You see how tall he is?

There were also two other men in the distance behind the gunman on the poster, perhaps supporting actors, also Japanese, and from the proportions of their bodies, it was clear that the gunman was much taller than the others.

No doubt he's tall, I said and burst out laughing. The man in the photo suddenly transformed into an older version of himself, which was without doubt the man we saw that night: the man I thought looked like Alain Delon in *The Samurai.* I saw him shaking his right hand, as if he were firing a gun.

What do you think you'll do? I asked.

I'll look for him in Japan.

It's crazy.

It may be, Elena said. Your lawyer will help me.

My lawyer?

Yes, Miryam. You were late today, Ricardo, and I arrived half an hour early to the gallery. I thought the show began at six—you know how I am with timings; sometimes I get them confused. In any case, Miryam came at the same time, and we started to talk. Did you know that she also didn't know her real father?

Did you talk about her father?

First we talked about art. I was surprised she knew so much of the contemporary scene; she knows several important artists, mostly women. Your lawyer is a woman full of surprises. Did you know she helped organize the exhibit?

I didn't know, I said. I thought the staff at the Mexican nonprofit did everything.

Almost everything, Elena replied. Your lawyer took care of the invitations and processed the paperwork for the visas; some of the artists had never been to the United States. The woman who did the woodcuts of missing women in Ciudad Juárez had never been outside of Mexico; it was her first time on a plane. Go figure!

I did know about her, I said. She's part of the team that we are working with in Mexico; she's also a lawyer, very committed to her work with the missing women. Oh, and Miryam is my *boss*, I added. She's never been my lawyer.

Elena looked me in the eye as if she'd suddenly remembered something and undid the bun of her hair, which she'd again dyed indigo blue. The dim light that came from the art deco lamps made it look darker, almost black and shiny, especially at the roots.

Whatever, Elena said fixing her bangs with her hand; she'd noticed my pointed gaze. The fact is, that at some point she asked me what drove me to paint, and I told her it was a way to fill a hole I've always felt within. Your lawyer—your boss—asked whether it was a family matter, and I said yes, and told her the whole story with plenty of details. She listened carefully and then told me that her story was similar. As a child and as a teenager, she'd also felt an emptiness within; her father was adoptive, and her mother almost never mentioned her real father—let's say her *biological* father, whom she later discovered she physically resembled, an astonishing likeness, apparently.

Elena fell silent and looked beyond me to the street. By the sound of it, I gathered that a group of people had entered the bar. We were across the street from the Curran Theatre; the evening function was over and some of the people in the audience came in to have a drink and perhaps also to wait for actors and other members of the cast; the place was a well-known hangout for theater people.

And how is this that she's going to help you? I asked, pulling my bar stool closer to hers. There was now a growing racket—new customers talking noisily, waiters moving about, doors opening and closing, the bartender busy serving drinks.

Your boss—Miryam—told me that she has some contacts in Japan who could help me find my father, Elena said, a slight frown on her face. She said she's working on a case with several lawyers in Tokyo. I guess you know about this, right?

Not much, I replied. I know it's about a property in Macau. I think I've told you something about this. Her client and the lawyers are Japanese. I imagine they work with private detectives or with the police; I don't know the details of the case, but perhaps she'll tell me later, if necessary; the only thing I know is that I'll have to translate into English some Portuguese documents. Anyway, I'm glad Miryam is willing to help you.

Me too, said Elena, tapping the bar with her hand, perhaps to add emphasis. She said that she would write a letter of introduction explaining that it was about finding my father. She was surprised when I told her I was going to be working in Tokyo from next February. She didn't know. She asked me what would happen to our relationship.

She asked you that?

Well, not immediately, Elena replied, looking at me sideways, perhaps she'd noticed my surprise. First, she asked what you thought about it. I told her I didn't know, and she very tactfully interceded for you; she said that you would likely talk to me about it soon, that she thought you thought things *through*. Elena said this last word in a sarcastic tone; I was expecting something like that.

That's what I wanted to talk about today, I said. Don't think I haven't thought things through. I know your trip is inevitable, and I understand why you have to go. I also understand that working in the language school is the most practical way forward. You won't have to teach more than twenty hours a week, and you'll have time to look for your father. If you were on a tourist visa, you would be limited to three months, and it would cost you a fortune.

What I want to know is what you are thinking of doing, Elena said, looking into my eyes.

I could go to visit, I said, knowing it was probably the worst answer I could give at the time. I'd thought about that scenario in the last few days, but I'd told myself that a young relationship like ours would never survive it. Elena kept looking intently at me; she had perhaps thought the same and had come to the same conclusion.

Or, you could come with me for a few months as a tourist and decide on the go whether you'd want to stay, Elena said.

I don't know if that's possible, I said. I mean—I corrected myself—I'm not sure it's a good idea for me to go with you at the end of February. I could go later, I don't know, after a few months, when things are more clear.

When they're clearer to you, Elena said.

When they're clearer to the two of us, I replied.

More convenient for you. You place your bets *very carefully*. Elena's tone was calm and mechanical, but she raised her voice slightly to say the last two words.

I said nothing and took a long drink of my beer. I

needed it; my throat was dry. Elena's attitude reminded me of my conversation with Veronique the day we had lunch at the Mexican *taqueria* near the office. I figured the two had talked about how I would react and respond to questions about my plans for the future, when the time came. I felt trapped but also aware that if I did not handle the situation well I would say something I might regret later. I had also thought of this second scenario that Elena had just mentioned, but my intuition had told me that it wouldn't work: I couldn't see myself idle in a foreign country on a hunt for a ghost that had nothing to do with me. On the other hand—what weighed more when I thought about it with a cool head—going to Japan, even for a short time, could jeopardize my work with the lawyers. Not only because I could lose my job—they could replace someone like me easily—but also because I could lose the opportunity to turn that job into a *career*. In the last two weeks, I'd again thought of an idea I'd before thought absurd: the possibility of studying law, of becoming a lawyer.

Give me a few days to think it over, I said. I had to repeat myself because Elena didn't hear me. Someone had said something in a loud voice behind us, something I did not understand but made the bartender, who was looking in that direction, burst out laughing. I've got to talk with Miryam and the other lawyers about my work in the coming months, I went on. Please remember that I have a temporary contract with the option to renew. And there's something else. I haven't told you anything yet, but I've been thinking about going to law school. It's just an idea, perhaps a crazy idea.

Elena looked at me puzzled, a faint smile on her lips. I'm not surprised to hear that, she said. It makes sense since you're working with lawyers…I don't know; I'm sure you'll figure it out. I don't know what else to say right now. The noise is driving me crazy.

A large group of people had come into the bar from the theater, I'd seen them cross the street when Elena was speaking, and the racket was becoming unbearable. One of the actors—you could tell by the way people greeted him—sat next to me at the bar, and in a matter of seconds, two fans came over to ask him for an autograph.

We'd better go home, I said and signaled the bartender for the check. Waiting for the change, I felt bad about what I said to Elena, and for the way I said it. I figured I'd disappointed her, that she expected better of me. It remained to be seen if I could be the person she needed now and in the future; I didn't know yet. It also remained to be seen if I had what it took to be a lawyer. It was the first time I'd told anyone what until now had been an idea in my mind, an abstraction. At the moment, the only thing that was real was Elena's trip, and the possibility that I would never see her again.

When we left, an icy wind ran down the street. Elena took my arm and we both walked in silence, our heads down to avoid the wind. We had not reached the first corner down the street when we saw an empty taxi, and we raised our hands at the same time to hail it. We rarely gave in to this kind of luxury; we always preferred to take public transportation or to walk, even if we were on the other side of the city.

There was a small traffic jam at Union Square crossing, where a crane was unloading a gigantic pine, the Christmas tree that would be placed in the center of the square; they were beginning to dress the city up for the year-end celebrations.

NINE

December flew by. I was busy the first two weeks with the translation from Portuguese to English, which turned out to be a lengthy legal file from a court in Macau on which I spent many hours at the office and several sleepless nights at home. The remaining two weeks, Miryam was sick with bronchitis, which coincided with Elena's trip to Los Angeles to see her mother; she said she did this every year. To pass my free time, I studied for the law school admission exam. I had thought about this before; Miryam had encouraged me to do it, but I had not had the time.

Elena came back from her trip the day before Christmas, and we spent a lot of time with our friends, celebrating the holidays or just hanging out together like we used to do when we lived at the Ansonia. Lisa and Veronique insisted we have dinner at their place nearly every evening, and on a couple of occasions we spent the night there; they had a tiny guest bedroom and sleeping bags.

Elena and I did not have much time to talk about us. We were in a kind of limbo where we had a good time as long as we did not touch on the topic of our impending separation. I got the impression that the two of us were expecting of the other a dramatic change of mind: on my part, that Elena would cancel her trip to Japan, and from hers, that I would agree to go with her.

One early January afternoon, we finally found ourselves without any plans to see our friends or go to an art opening or to the movies as we usually did on weekend afternoons. We were relaxing on the couch in the living room of Elena's apartment; her cat Neko was purring on my lap.

I was turning around in my head ideas as to how to approach the topic we were avoiding: how to bring it up, what turn of phrase to use; I didn't want any misunderstandings, but I couldn't make up my mind. I dismissed all the phrases that came to mind; they seemed too direct. Instead, I opted to tell her that I had applied to take the law school entrance examination in June.

Elena turned to look at me a little surprised. I guess this is your way of telling me that you're definitely not going with me to Tokyo, she said in a tone that seemed carefree, although I noticed a trace of irritation.

I've told you about the test at least twice: when we spoke on the phone, and when you were at your mom's,

I reminded her.

You told me you were studying, not that you were going to take the test. Elena got up to say that and lit a cigarette.

It follows that if I'm studying, it is to take the test, I said.

Don't change the subject now, Ricardo. What's clear to me is that you've already made up your mind not to go to Japan.

We'd already talked about it, I said.

What I remember is that you were going to Tokyo for a few weeks and then would decide on the go whether you wanted to stay or not.

All this time, I've been telling you that I've been thinking seriously about going to law school.

Yes, but you always tell me what you're *thinking*, not what you're going to do.

Taking the test doesn't guarantee that I'll do well or get accepted into law school.

I have no doubt that you'll do well. When you set your mind on something you get it. Elena was standing with her back to me, looking at something out the window. In the sky, there were rows of thick and bulging clouds that quickly changed shape and moved toward the bay.

Berkeley has an excellent law school, I said.

And if you don't get in?

We'll see, I said. There are other law schools in the Bay Area.

I see you've given it some thought, Ricardo, Elena said, her back still to me.

I felt bad then; the conversation wasn't going the way I'd hoped. I thought it would have been better to wait until she'd taken up the topic herself. The night before at the neighborhood Thai restaurant, where we went when we didn't feel like cooking, Elena had been about to mention it. She was saying something about Veronique's parents coming to see her before the trip, but she suddenly changed the subject to tell me she'd met a potential buyer for the new whirlwind painting: a former art teacher, and that it seemed a done deal, and she did not go back to talking about Veronique or the trip for the rest of the evening.

Elena turned around quietly and came back to the couch, next to me. She stubbed out her cigarette in the ashtray on the coffee table—she'd hardly smoked it halfway—and took a deep breath, or it was rather a long sigh.

I was afraid of this, she said.

I didn't say I wouldn't go to see you.

Would they give you holidays at work? Elena sounded surprised; perhaps she had not thought it possible. Me neither, actually; Miryam had told me only a few days ago that I could take vacation time between contracts, though without pay.

If they renew my contract, I could take a couple of weeks between June and July, I said.

Elena put both hands on her temples, as she did when she felt a headache coming, but she withdrew them quickly.

Better than nothing, she said.

By that time, you might want to come back.

It's possible, she replied. It all depends on whether I find my father.

You know what I think about that, I said.

I know you think it's crazy to look for him. Elena spoke now in a low voice, as if musing to herself. I think I've spent my life trying to be a person I can't be, she went on, her voice growing louder. I mean, I've spent my life as the person my mother wants me to be: sweet, hardworking, stable. But, what I've always felt is that I've got to get away, go somewhere else, be different. It's like a yearning that I've always repressed.

You can figure that out by yourself, or perhaps through therapy, I said, and I regretted it instantly. I remembered that Elena had told me that in high school she had to see a psychologist for her aggressive behavior toward her classmates—which she said was her way of defending herself against being harassed by them—and it had seemed a waste of time. It was the others who needed therapy, she'd told me; she just wanted to be left alone.

Elena shook her head and looked into my eyes. You don't understand me, she said. I feel that part of me is like my father, or at least how I imagine him from what Mom tells me: intense, impulsive, emotional, but also creative. It's also clear to me that he's selfish, or may not think much about everyone else, or doesn't care, or thinks that people should take care of themselves the best way they can. I don't know. As for me, I've tried not to be that way. What do you think?

You're not like that, I said. Intense and impulsive, yes; selfish, no.

But, I'm difficult. I don't know how you put up with me.

I don't think that, but if you say so.

Elena jokingly pushed my arm. I think that I started to live my own life when I went to art school, she went on. Before that, school was torture for me; I felt I was enrolled at a correctional facility. I was always fighting with Mom because of my bad temper and my way of being so unpredictable. I think that if I get to know my father, I'll be able to know myself better and avoid making the mistakes he's made. I know it sounds weird. And besides, keep in mind that I'm half-Japanese.

What does that mean? I laughed a little despite myself.

I don't know. That I'll feel at home in Japan?

You don't inherit your culture, I said.

I know, don't be silly. What I mean is that it'll be easier for me to get used to Japanese culture. Besides, you know I like Japanese art, and I speak the language a little.

Elena raised her eyebrows as she said that and looked at her bookshelves. Then she closed her eyes, as if she were tired; perhaps she had not slept well or indeed had a headache. She was getting them quite often lately.

At least you have Japanese blood, I said.

What do you mean?

Nothing. Sorry. I was thinking of my father.

You say that he thinks he's English, right? Elena sat back on the couch, and I turned to face her.

Something like that. Dad says his family comes from Navarra in northern Spain, but that their ancestors were Celts.

And you don't think he has any Celt in him?

The liver. He drinks a lot of whiskey.

But there's nothing Celtic about you, Elena said and let out what I thought was a sarcastic laugh, which was not usual for her. You're darker than me, and your frizzy hair…

I'll tell you a little something about my family, I said. Dad is very white—pink, I'd say. He turns red easily when he's in a bad mood, also with a few glasses of whiskey. His wavy hair was also a little red when he was young; it's now very white, almost platinum. All that he inherited from my grandfather. If you see pictures of both them at fifty, they're identical. My grandmother was a little less pink, but also white—pale, I'd say—with light brown eyes, like Dad. Mom and her family, on the other hand, are quite different. She's got cinnamon skin and black eyes, like me. Her hair is straight and shiny, like yours.

And your brother?

He looks like Mom and me, but he's like my father.

I don't get it.

They don't look alike, except they're both tall; taller than me. What I mean is that my brother's temperament is like my father's: arrogant and intolerant, and he gets angry easily. Apart from that, he wants to be like him: wealthy and conservative, like the Republicans here.

Is he interested in politics?

I don't think so. But he likes money and power.

He studied business at a university in Bogotá and is now doing a master's in finance. In London, of course.

I see he's not your favorite person, Elena said and gave me a look of slight concern.

You see what kind of a dysfunctional family, I have, I said, adding, and that's all I can tell you now.

In that case, let's get back to my stuff. I spoke to Miryam on Friday afternoon. Her contacts in Japan told her that it's very difficult to find someone like my father. They need more information. Apparently, there are dozens of men with that exact name. She told me that I need to find out exactly when and where he was born.

Does your mom know any of this?

She knows when he was born but not exactly where. She remembers he was from Tokyo, but not the name of the neighborhood. What she *likes* to remember is that he was very handsome, tall, and with bristling hair. And, that when he laughed, his cheeks rose: he has unusually high cheekbones. She told me that when I went to see her a few weeks ago.

Perhaps he was into Botox, I said.

Don't joke with this, Ricardo.

And of his movies? I asked.

As an actor he didn't make any other movies, at least nothing known. The studio where he worked went bankrupt—or rather, a larger studio took it over—and they have no record of him. Miryam promised me she would dig a little more. It's funny. She also said something like what you just said: that perhaps my father had had plastic surgery. Actors often do that to keep looking young. But I don't know what kind of procedures they did back then; it would have been the late sixties o early seventies, I think. I should find out on Internet or ask a doctor. Miryam said that her friends in Japan employ a detective for some research projects, and she'll ask them to add my father's name to the list of the people they're investigating. She also told me not to worry about the expense because they were investigating some other men of about the same age, and an additional name was not going to change the fee.

That night we went to Lisa and Veronique's place for dinner and to celebrate the one-month anniversary of Lydia and Felipe being together. According to Veronique, who had called me several times the last few days to keep me posted on the latest developments, Lydia and Felipe had recently decided to go together to Japan and were already doing the paperwork with contracts and visas.

That they were now in a relationship did not surprise me. Since we met at the Ansonia, I noticed that the two liked each other: Felipe was always looking for ways to approach Lydia at dinnertime or when we went out for a drink, and she always seemed nicer to him, more considerate; Lydia tends to be a little unfriendly with people who don't share her views and opinions. The problem they had—which they had the first time they dated—was communication. Neither of them spoke English well back then, and it was evident that during the short time they were together, things did not work out because of plain misunderstandings. According to Veronique, this time they had both promised to be patient and to talk over everything with cool heads. Besides, by this time, they both spoke much better English.

What surprised me was that the two of them were planning to go to Japan. I had figured that Lydia was thinking about it and had contacted the Alliance Française or the recruiter from the language school in Tokyo, but I had not imagined that Felipe would also be interested.

Of the two, I was going to miss Felipe more. Apart from Mom, he was the only person I spoke Spanish with.

When we got to their place, Felipe opened the door and greeted me with a tight hug.

We're going to miss you very much, he said.

Me too. I did not know what else to say. I felt desolate, as if instead of being there I was reliving a memory.

In the living room, Lydia was serving a round of champagne glasses for everyone.

We toasted the happy couple, the upcoming trip, and our friendship. When we sat to eat, I was feeling a bit hot—perhaps it was the heating that was set high—and not so much desolate as mildly depressed. I was living the moment when I saw all my friends about to leave the city. Elena squeezed my hand under the table, as if she had noticed my reaction.

After dinner, we had shots of limoncello and went back to the living room.

Veronique took her laptop to the coffee table and after searching for something in the Internet, asked us to come over and look.

A couple of days ago, Javier Pinto sent me the link of the building where we're going to live, she said.

All together? I asked. I felt a little confused; I could not remember anyone telling me anything about living arrangements in Tokyo. I suddenly remembered our days at the Ansonia—quick images flashing in my head—and how nice it was to know that my friends lived in the same building, and that I could see them very often.

In two apartments, Lisa said, and cast a side-glance at Elena. As Elena has probably told you, she's going to live with us, she added. That way, we can all save more money. Look, she said pointing to the screen and turning to me—the others may have seen it before—our apartment has two bedrooms. It looks large, by Japanese standards, I mean.

On the webpage that Veronique opened appeared a picture of a furnished room with a double bed and a desk, then one of another bedroom with two single beds, a dresser, and two desks. To the right of the second room, a window was visible, and through it, in the distance, there was a skyscraper of futuristic design with rounded edges, probably an office building. It was an evening scene; the city looked scattered in the distance, points of light on the horizon.

What about Felipe and Lydia's? Elena asked.

It's not yet available, Felipe said.

Pinto said it was on a lower floor, but with the same view. It seems that the current tenants will leave in a month, Lisa said.

And this guy, Pinto—is he is reliable? I asked in the most neutral tone I could muster. I had heard his name mentioned so many times in the recent months that already developed an aversion to him; I considered him to be an intruder, responsible for the departure of my friends.

Pinto has done everything well, Lisa said. Our contracts and the visas arrived on the date he announced. I have no reason to doubt him.

He's also done everything efficiently for us, Lydia said. He had to rush the process because we would like to go together with Lisa and Veronique and start working at the same time, and so far, everything has gone well. Next week, I have an appointment at the Japanese consulate for the visa. Felipe's contract is going to take longer, as well as his visa. It seems they don't have Spanish courses starting all the time. But Pinto said that as far as the visa was concerned, it was not a problem, because Felipe could change his tourist visa for a work visa, and they would open Spanish courses in May or June at the school. So there's no reason to worry.

Pinto sent me more information, Veronique said, and sat on the floor in front of her laptop. In this website, she said after clicking on a link (probably from some list that Pinto had sent her), there's information about the neighborhood where we'll live. It looks like it's mixed residential and commercial. There are clinics, banks, beauty salons, restaurants, bars, and clubs nearby. While she said that, Veronique opened and closed webpages. At that moment, I thought of the word "windows" and I saw through them a dental clinic, a branch of a US bank, an Indian restaurant, another Mexican, a Latino club with an announcement of salsa and merengue classes on the door, and others.

Veronique returned to the window of the Latin club; something caught her attention and also mine: the photos. Veronique enlarged several of them: they were typical scenes of bars and clubs: people toasting with drinks, and couples dancing. There were Japanese and foreigners, especially Latin Americans, judging by their faces. Some of them had Asian features, probably a half or a third Japanese; I knew that there were many Latinos of Japanese ancestry in Japan.

Looking closely at one of the photos, I noticed an attractive young woman of cinnamon skin and curly hair, who smiled, amused with her partner on the dance floor, and the image of my cousin Adriana came back to me. I remembered that I danced with her several times at an end-of-the-year party we hosted at home; maybe it was then that I fell in love with her. That night she told me she wanted to travel and see the world, and that as soon as she could she would. Adriana was older than me by three or four years and was far more experienced. Where was she now?

TEN

After Elena and my friends left for Japan, my life changed drastically. It was like a sudden and rude awakening from a pleasant dream, in which I was certain that everything was going well, to a reality that seemed flat and full of uncertainty. I spent most of the day at the office, which had become my second home, the only space where I had contact with other people. I was almost always the first to arrive, and the last to leave—from my section, I mean; the lawyers often worked late, sometimes spending the night in their offices. When I completed the projects that they assigned me or had some free time, I went to the firm's library to study. I liked that quiet room with its comfortable armchairs and leather sofas, the floor-to-ceiling bookcases, and the spectacular view of San Francisco Bay.

On weekend mornings, I walked around the city. I would usually take one of the main trails of Golden Gate Park, from the Panhandle just across the street from my building. Along the way, I would ponder how much my life had changed since I moved to the city. I often thought of the advantages that came from being a US citizen and not having to return to Bogotá, to my family's world and their expectations, especially my father's. Although I missed Elena and my friends, who had become my family, I knew it was something temporary. If I couldn't get into a good law school, I would have the option to go to Japan, though I would have to think about that carefully, but I would still have a good job at the firm if I didn't become a lawyer. I would walk through the park without haste, enjoying the fresh morning air. I liked to go to the building by the cliff, where there is a restaurant and bar, and look at the Pacific Ocean; the sound of the waves crashing against the rocks below soothed me and put my mind at ease.

Other days, I explored neighborhoods I didn't know. I would walk up and down their streets, go in the shops and bookstores to look and browse for a while, and have lunch at one of the local restaurants. In the afternoons, and sometimes the evenings, I went to the movies, to the downtown cinemas where they showed foreign films. I would watch whatever they had on, sometimes two movies in a row. In the evenings, I usually went to dinner at any of the Asian restaurants in my neighborhood, Thai, Japanese, and Vietnamese;

then at home, I would have a couple of beers and study a few hours for the LSAT until I fell asleep.

Nothing had changed at home; my roommates kept their night schedules and spent the weekends with their girlfriends, at our place or theirs. When I felt lonely, I would call my family in Colombia and talk to Mom for a long time. Dad was always busy; he would come to the phone for a bit to ask me the usual things: if I liked my work, how much money I made, whether I was saving enough, and things like that. I hadn't told him that I intended to go to law school. I wanted it to be a surprise, when the time came.

The first few weeks, I talked to Elena almost every day: on the phone at first and then almost always on Skype, sometimes twice a day, depending on Elena's schedule; that first month was chaotic with her new job. Besides, the time difference was sixteen hours, so that often one of us was either about to go to sleep or had just gotten up. After the first three weeks, when everything was new for her, we started to talk every other day, and our conversations fell in a pattern along the lines of those from our weekly routine in San Francisco: complaints about work and gossip about our friends, who were still very much part of our lives, now more than ever because they all lived in the same place as her, though I only chatted with them once in a while, on the rare occasions when they were all at home, and Elena happened to be in the living room.

One morning, Elena called me to tell me she had a new clue about her father. I had not yet woken up; it took me a few seconds to turn on the bedside lamp and realize that my computer was right there; I had studied late.

His family is from a place called Isehara, she said in the tone she used for big news.

How do you know that? I rubbed my eyes to wake myself up.

From the detective agency, Elena replied. I already told you that they'd found his personnel file in the studios where he made his films in the sixties, though it had no personal information other than a phone number that no longer works. But they dug deeper in the Tokyo archives and found that a man with that name had been sued for not paying back a loan and left that phone number as his family's contact in Isehara.

So, Ibuke-san had a police record, I said. A few days ago, Elena started to refer to her father in the Japanese style, surname first, followed by *san*; she did not like Hiroki, his first name. This was also customary at the language school with the foreign teachers, though not in Elena's case. Ogawa-san, the middle-aged bald man we met at the Nikko Hotel in San Francisco, who turned out to be the director and general manager, insisted that everyone call her Rita-san, in homage to Rita Hayworth, one of his favorite movie stars, whom he said Elena resembled, not only in bearing but also in personality. I thought this was a bit weird, not to say inappropriate, but Elena had no problem with it; she happily agreed, and said it had some truth in it.

Elena had, in fact, seen many of Rita Hayworth's movies—she had a small DVD collection of them—and considered herself one of her fans. But she wasn't interested in Rita Hayworth because she liked classic Hollywood movies, but because she'd been intrigued by her life and work after we went to see *Mulholland Drive*, a film by David Lynch in which one of the protagonists, a young woman who suffers from amnesia, realizes that she has an extraordinary resemblance to her. I hadn't seen any of those old movies, but thanks to Elena leaving me her collection, I was watching them now. Last night I'd watched *Gilda*, one of her most famous movies, which surprised me several times because in some dramatic closeup shots, Gilda's gaze was indeed like Elena's, her expressive brown eyes also large and almond-shaped.

It seems that Ibuke-san is, or was, as bad as Mom imagines, Elena said and squinted in front of the camera, perhaps trying to see my face; I had moved a little.

I'm not up yet, I said. I went to bed very late, almost at midnight. Did they tell you anything else? I drew the curtains to let the morning light in. I thought that knowing where his parents lived was an important clue, although perhaps they've already passed away.

They're working on it. In this country, everything is complicated; there's a lot of paperwork, even for the most trivial things. One of the detectives is at the city registry in Isehara right now.

Will they charge you for this?

Not yet. The detective agency will send me the bill at the end of the month, but they told me it wouldn't be too much, at most three hundred dollars.

Wow, I said. I hope they don't charge you more. So far, Elena's inquiries had been for free. Miryam made it so that our firm covered the expenses if the queries overlapped with the research we were doing at the Tokyo city registry.

Don't you have classes today? I asked. It was Wednesday, and Elena taught some of her classes in the evening.

Today's a national holiday. We're going to a Peruvian restaurant nearby. This neighborhood has everything! Every week we discover a new restaurant or bar. Do you want to come? They say that their ceviche is out of this world.

I'd love to, but you know how it is at the office.

You tell me every day, Elena quipped.

We're moving on with the Macau case, which gets more complicated by the day, I said. I must thoroughly check the file of one of the Macau counterclaimants, a man in his late seventies. It seems that he's got a bank account in San Francisco and some businesses in the United States, something that suits us well because we can look into his financial records; Miryam thinks there's something fishy there. There are also Japanese ties every which way. The old man's lawyer is Japanese; he has his office in Yokohama. According to Miryam, he has some connections with yakuza gangsters—nothing conclusive, apparently, just speculation, but she believes we should investigate further.

Sounds like detective's work, Elena said.

Our firm has become like a detective's office. We investigate miscreants and document their villainy.

Miscreants and their villainy? Who talks like that?

You can't imagine how much time I spend with my dictionaries at work.

Will you come to Japan to investigate the lawyer? Elena's eyes narrowed again, maybe there wasn't yet enough light in the room. The morning was overcast as far as I could see through the window.

Miryam will take care of that, I said. It's not paralegal work.

But you could ask her, right?

Sure, I'll try, I replied without much conviction. I didn't think Miryam would take me seriously if I asked if I could join the Macau research team that was going to Japan with her. I was just beginning to understand my new job. I'd formally joined the paralegal team three weeks before thanks to my preparing to take the law school admission test. What I'm working on is going to take a lot of time, six weeks at the minimum, I hastily added, to better explain myself. There are four or five boxes of documents in Portuguese. Luckily, I must only translate what pertains to the marriage and divorce of a couple and the division of their assets. Some of the documents are from the 1940s, Rita Hayworth's days, so the laws were quite different. I think Miryam will be traveling in three weeks or so, I pointed out.

Will she come to Tokyo?

She has not confirmed it, but I think so. Or, maybe Yokohama. But they are near each other, right?

Next to each other, actually. I already told you that we went to Yokohama's Chinatown one afternoon.

Yes, and you had a great time; I know.

Did I tell you that Felipe met some Mexicans there?

You told me that Javier Pinto had some Mexican

friends there, I said.

The same people. Pinto knows all kinds of people everywhere. Elena said, dropping her voice to a whisper, as if there was some mystery in that bit of information. He's an odd guy, she went on. He only works with Ogawa at the time of recruiting teachers, as a sort of consultant. Felipe told me that he'd told him he was a journalist, and occasionally wrote pieces on controversial topics, but he didn't say where he worked or published his articles, or if it was freelancing, like his gig with the language school.

Suddenly someone knocked on the door.

It means that Lisa and Veronique are ready to leave, Elena said with a frown of regret. Felipe and Lydia are also waiting. They send you hugs. We'll talk later, OK? I've got to go. Don't forget to read my last report. A big kiss, she said with a pout of her lips, and finished the call from her side.

Elena's reports were like journal entries documenting everything about the search for her father. At first, I didn't pay much attention to those long emails filled with information about public archives, police departments, and the like, which seemed to me futile or banal. Elena had told me that I didn't have to comment, but I couldn't help but imagine she expected exactly the opposite from me; that it was a way to make me part of her quest.

When I looked at the computer screen, I realized that it was only a quarter past six. Elena had forgotten not to call so early; the recent daylight saving time change in San Francisco had mixed us up. We figured it the other way around: instead of an hour earlier for her, it was an hour earlier for me.

I was about to go back to sleep when the image of the samurai came to my memory, the man we saw that night on our way to the blues club, who could be Ibuke. I lay back on the bed and tried to imagine him, to form an idea of what kind of man he could be.

If Elena was right and he'd been an actor, maybe connected in some way with the yakuza at the time, what kind of business would he be in now? Did he become a respectable businessman, like the executives we saw at the Nikko Hotel? Or a career criminal? A con man?

I knew very little about Japanese society to be able to speculate. Apart from a historical novel I'd read years ago, something about Japanese Christians, and a Haruki Murakami collection of short stories that someone gave me in college, I didn't know anything about Japanese literature. I'd never been interested; not because of some personal bias, but because I simply didn't have the time. I didn't know much about Japanese cinema either. I'd seen several Kurosawa classics, and recently more contemporary ones, following the advice of the book I had bought about Japanese cinema, but they hadn't been enough to give me an idea of what kind of man Ibuke could be.

In a downtown video store, I'd bought two movies about the yakuza, but they hadn't helped much. Some of the characters had left me puzzled, like Takeshi Kitano's in *Fireworks*, about a former police detective who has problems with the Mafia. This was a very violent man, in a bizarre way, but perhaps I just didn't get it. Besides, the quintessential bandit for me was still Alain Delon in *The Samurai*. It was a difficult role to forget: his dedication to crime, his loyalty to the code of the underworld, his silence.

The movies had also not helped me get a good idea of Tokyo, or at least of the neighborhood where Elena lived. You couldn't see Tokyo tower in any of them, which Elena said was behind her building, though several blocks away, or the famous entertainment districts with foreign bars and clubs that Elena often mentioned, which I imagined along the lines of North Beach and Chinatown in San Francisco.

I wondered what kind of detectives worked for our firm in Tokyo. Until then, I never had anything to do with detectives, or met or been acquainted with one, or even with someone who knew one or had used their services. For me, the detective had always been a fictional character, from the Ellery Queen novels we had in our library at home in Bogotá, or from *film noir*; I didn't like the ones from TV series, they all seemed cut from the same fabric to me. It had not occurred to me that they could be ordinary people, employees like me, who earned their living by investigating the lives of strangers, rummaging through their secrets, and documenting their misdeeds.

I couldn't sleep, though I didn't have to get up until seven so I could get to the office before eight-thirty. The business with the detectives was still spinning in my head, now tangled up with things Mom told me last week. When I told her that Elena was in contact with the detectives who were looking for traces of her father, she asked me if they could help me contact Adriana, my second-degree cousin, who once again had not sent word of how she was or of her whereabouts.

Sofía, Adriana's mother, Mom's cousin, was very worried. A stranger had phoned her to tell her—in a threatening tone—that the next time she talked to her daughter, she should remind her that she had outstanding obligations to those who had financed her trip to Japan.

I told Mom that they should wait a couple of weeks; perhaps Adriana had again changed jobs and moved and was not yet ready to get in touch. I promised her that I would ask Miryam about the detectives; after all, it could be a case of human rights violations.

I thought again of the detectives who gave Elena the report about her father, and for some reason one of them was Takeshi Kitano, the Japanese actor in *Fireworks.* He was telling me something, not just with words but with his face, which changed expressions from sadness to anger, or so it seemed to me. I understood that he was lost, his life was a disaster, and he saw no way out. While I pondered that, I realized that I was dreaming; I'd fallen asleep with the computer on my lap.

ELEVEN

In the following weeks, the work in the office became more intense. The lawyers hired several additional part-time paralegals to help with Miryam's case, which, as per the rumor mill at the office, had more edges and complications with each passing day.

One afternoon toward the end of the week, I was taken by surprise by Miryam, who was waiting for me at my cubicle when I came back from lunch break. She invited me to dinner; she said she had something important to talk to me about. It was unusual for her to come and see me; she usually would contact me by email, or call me on the phone if it was urgent. It occurred to me that it would have to be something about Elena, a breakthrough in the investigation of her father's whereabouts, or perhaps some bad news, the man was in prison or had died. I said yes, and we agreed on seven o'clock at a restaurant near the office where they sometimes took clients for a meal.

There are a couple of things we need to discuss, Miryam said in the formal tone she used in the office after we placed our order. They gave us a table with a view of Market Street, which was very busy; the downtown rush-hour traffic was not yet over.

I'm all ears, I replied. Miryam looked a little agitated or upset and had a scowl on her face. She wore a cotton scarf around her neck, which she took off in haste; it got entangled in her ponytail. Perhaps she was feeling too warm; the weather was changing those days, and it was unpredictable.

As you well know, the case we have in Macau has gotten complicated, Miryam continued, finally free of the scarf. It's now clear to us that it's related to many other things we're interested in, even with some that we had not anticipated. By coincidence, one of them is related to Elena's search for her father, and perhaps with other things that might interest you.

I figured something like that would happen when you suggested that Elena use the same detective office in Tokyo, I said.

That's where the coincidence came from, Miryam said. When Elena gave me the little information she had about her father, I realized that I'd seen that name somewhere. I looked through the electronic files of the Macau case, which you know are very extensive—luckily it's quite easy with the new search engine they installed—and found that someone with that same name was a shareholder of one of the companies represented by the Japanese lawyer in Yokohama, the same lawyer we are investigating.

Was the company a movie studio?

Yes, Miryam smiled halfheartedly, her expression more relaxed now. I see Elena already told you.

I nodded. Do you think that lawyer knows the whereabouts of Elena's father?

It's possible, Miryam replied. But for the time being, we're not interested in that man. I have no reason to think that he is involved in what we're investigating. You never know, of course. We'll see. For now, we need to focus on the lawyer. I suspect he is just a front man and that there are other, more important characters behind him. In fact, we have some clues that it's so. We know he represents several businessmen we have in the crosshairs; but we have nothing solid; it's a very complex case. I think the property suit in Macau is just the tip of a gigantic iceberg, and there are many submerged things that we could bring up.

Will the firm take over the investigation?

Yes, one of the new paralegals, Shigeru, a young Japanese guy we hired last month just for this case, will travel to Tokyo tonight and do some initial research.

When she finished saying this, Miryam turned on her mobile phone, next to her glass of wine, and glanced at the hour.

What we suspect is that one of the businesses, a company formerly related to the film studios, is involved with the trafficking of women to Japan, she added. We already knew some things through our client in Macau, but we are still not sure if there is a direct connection.

Wasn't the trafficking of women in Macau? I was sure that Miryam had told me that at some point. I'd also recently read an Internet article on the subject and its connection to money laundering and illegal gambling.

In Macau and Japan, Miryam said. As I told you before, Macau is a trafficking hub. The local organized crime has ties with the Japanese yakuza, who bring women to Japan to work in the sex industry.

I didn't know that the Japanese Mafia had business in other countries, I said. To mind came a scene from Takeshi Kitano's movie *Fireworks* that had left an impression on me, in which a yakuza gang gives a friend of the protagonist a horrible beating that leaves him paralyzed.

It's a long story, said Miryam. You'll get all the details as you get to work on this project. In fact, you'll have to work exclusively on this case in the coming months. We'll put our Spanish classes on hold. I hope that doesn't bother you.

Not at all, I answered. It'll be a pleasure to work on this. You know this interests me.

I'm glad to hear that, she said, and eyed me sideways. I thought she was going to ask me something, but the waiter arrived with our order.

While they served us seafood dishes and vegetables, Miryam looked out of the window at the ferry terminal's clock tower, only a couple of blocks away. A shiny-green 1950s tram with yellow stripes was passing in front of it. Along with the wrought-iron lamps of the street, it gave the urban landscape a curious air of yesteryear.

The important thing for us, Miryam went on, is to uncover the links between the companies that the Japanese lawyer represents and the trafficking of women to Japan. It's something that may interest you personally, she added with some emphasis.

I'm not sure I follow you, I said. It occurred to me that Miryam was referring to Adriana, my third cousin, though that was unlikely. I made a quick account of the things I'd said to Miryam about her, but it hadn't been much: just that she lived in Japan and perhaps had been deceived about the terms of her work contract.

Did Elena tell you something? I asked.

Yes, I hope it wasn't something private, Miryam said.

No, it isn't private. What exactly did she tell you?

That your cousin could be the victim of female trafficking in Japan.

It's possible, I said. Her mother, my mother's cousin, is very worried about that. Me too, of course. She's a distant cousin, but it's my family, after all.

So, it does interest you.

I nodded and thought about the last conversation I had with Mom about the detectives. I decided not to say anything about it. It seemed to me that everything was going in that direction, and that sooner or later, we would talk about it.

I'd like to ask you to come to Japan with me as part of the research team, Miryam said, and looked me in the eye. I need you to help me with several things. One of them, perhaps the most important, is to interpret for me at meetings with some Latin American diplomats and journalists. The diplomats speak English well, but the journalists don't, and I want to make sure we all understand each other in the best way possible. What they tell us could help us confirm our suspicions. As you imagine, we'll have to document everything.

Yes, I accept, of course, I said.

You look surprised.

I didn't expect it. I thought I blushed a little; it happened sometimes, I couldn't help it. I'm really glad, I hastily added. I didn't want to give the impression that I hesitated.

Very well, Miryam said. You take a load off my mind. I wasn't sure you would accept. Did you already get your US passport?

Yes, I said, a few months ago. Elena's face came to my mind. We had gone to the post office together to apply for it; it was also the first time for her.

My assistant will take care of the rest. Cheers!

I'm very grateful, I said and lifted my glass.

By the way, how are your preparations for the exam going? Miryam sounded more casual, her face free of tension now.

So far so good. I've taken six practice exams, and my scores are good.

That's great. I think you've studied enough, though it wouldn't hurt to do another practice test. On this trip, we'll be in Japan two weeks or so, fifteen days at the most, so you'll have more than a week to recover from the trip before you take the June exam.

I'm intrigued by the journalists you mentioned.

As to why we're going to talk to them?

To begin with.

Again Miryam checked the time on her mobile

phone, perhaps thinking about the bus schedule for her suburb. There are two Peruvian journalists who've been investigating the trafficking of women to Japan for several years, she said. Since the early nineties, if I'm not mistaken. Back then, most of the women who were trafficked to Japan were Asian, Thai, and Filipino. Then, Latin American women started to come, mainly Colombian and Chilean—and Peruvian also, I think. The traffickers were, and are, mostly Japanese, but with the complicity and help of Latin American gangsters, both in Japan and in their countries.

Are there Latin American gangsters in Japan?

We'll find out all that during our trip, Miryam said. A few years ago, the Japanese authorities took drastic measures to put a stop to the trafficking of people; they even arrested a well-known Japanese trafficker. Unfortunately, it hasn't been enough. Nowadays, it's business as usual. I've read that many Mexican women have recently come to Japan, especially to Tokyo. We'll have to see if they're all victims.

Aren't they all victims?

That is a complicated subject as well. There is a Brazilian sociologist with whom we'll have to talk about it; she's published several articles on the trafficking of Latinas in Japan.

I wasn't expecting much academic interest, I said.

I don't know how much the scholars can help us, Miryam said, raising her eyebrows. They're often ensconced in their ivory towers, or further up on the moon.

After dinner, I walked Miryam to the bus station, just a few blocks from the restaurant. We'd finished the bottle of white wine and were both a little tipsy. On the way, we talked about Elena's search for her father. Miryam said she understood her very well; you couldn't ignore such things. It was always better to know. She told me that in her case, she'd met her biological father only a couple of years ago. She had to find him on her own because her mother always said she didn't know where he was.

When I asked her what it was like to have met him, she told me it had been strange, though in some way predictable. She'd felt comfortable right from the start and close to him in a way that resonated deep within her, as if he were an older, male version of herself. But then, she admitted, it was perhaps all wishful thinking, a sort of *projection* of her own longings; she'd have to give it more thought. She also added that meeting him had not given her the *answers* she wanted, though it had made her feel better, as if she had freed herself from a heavy burden because she now knew the truth of her origins, and had also learned something she had only intuited before: that there was someone else in the world who was like her. She was going to tell me something else, but at that moment her bus came, and she had to leave. She gave me a half hug. It was the first time she ever did that; she always greeted me and said goodbye with a handshake.

I took the first bus going in the general direction of my neighborhood, although it was not the most convenient route; I would have to walk for at least fifteen minutes. On the way, as I looked out the window (that night, for some reason I felt I was in a city I didn't know), I thought it unlikely that Elena would have the same experience as Miryam with her father because they lived in different countries with very different cultures. Unless you believed that it was all in the genes, which I found absurd—I was certain that I had not inherited anything from my father—but many people felt was true, perhaps Elena too.

As I brooded over that, I realized that we were passing through Japantown, near some of the restaurants where Elena and I had gone a few times in the past. We had also been a couple of times to one of the karaoke bars in the neighborhood with Lisa and Veronique, who loved singing 1980s oldies and sipping Japanese whisky. Felipe and Lydia could not stand karaoke, but Elena and I were indifferent and had gone along just for the pleasure of seeing our friends having fun. I felt a pang of nostalgia for those evenings. On one occasion, we stayed until closing time in the early morning and discovered common ground with David Bowie, singing his songs at the top of our lungs. I never felt as close to anyone in my life as I'd felt to Elena and Veronique.

The bus made one of its scheduled stops in front of the Kabuki Cinemas, and out of impulse I decided to get off. I wasn't in a hurry to get home.

I thought back on my dinner with Miryam. She was also someone with whom I'd felt a sort of kinship from the beginning. When we had a chance to talk, like we did tonight, it always felt to me like she was a sort of older, wiser sister, who gave me all kinds of advice and cared about me. I was happy that she asked me to go to Japan, not only because I would be able to see Elena and my friends, but because I would be working on a real case and learning the ropes of what I was hoping would be my profession in the future.

As I was reaching home, I imagined myself in four or five years. I was already one of the lawyers in the firm, with an office like Miryam's, overlooking the Bay Bridge. I was working on a complicated case like the one in Macau. But, it was in another country, perhaps in Spain or Portugal, something that had to do with immigrants or refugees, although I had not seen anything like it at the office; our clients were mostly from Mexico and Central America, some from Ecuador, with all the conflict between the multinational oil companies and the indigenous groups that lived near the oil fields in the rainforest. In that future I was still with Elena; perhaps we would be married then or simply living together. Each of us had a busy and successful life: I as an associate at the firm, Elena dedicated to her art, with frequent exhibitions in San Francisco and other cities, Tokyo, for example, or perhaps the owner of a downtown gallery.

PART TWO

ONE

Roppongi crossing was crowded with people waiting to cross the street, and others like me, standing under the awning of a coffee shop, waiting for friends or partners. According to Elena, the corner was a well-known meeting spot, a departure point to explore the nightlife of this part of the city. It was my first night in Tokyo, and I felt overwhelmed by the density and energy of the place. Judging from the neon signs that surrounded me, there were all sorts of businesses nearby: bars, dance clubs, restaurants, and others that offered a myriad of entertainment possibilities. A gigantic television screen across the street was showing a commercial for a line of cosmetics using speech bubbles of exclamations and explosions, like in comic books.

I was waiting for Elena. She told me on the phone earlier, at lunchtime, that she finished her classes at seven, ten minutes ago. The plan was to have dinner with our friends at a nearby restaurant and then spend the night together at my hotel. The weather was perfect, just like it was in San Francisco when I left—clear skies and a cool spring breeze.

Here I am, Elena whispered in my ear and gave me a kiss on the cheek. She was right next to me, perhaps for a few seconds, and I had not noticed. You look just like on Skype. She burst out laughing.

Dazed and confused, I replied, still shocked that I didn't see her arrive. For some reason, I had thought that the language school was on the other side of the crossing, like my hotel, a few blocks away. I would have to check my map and be careful not to get lost.

You always look a little dazed and confused, she said and gave me a tight hug. Elena looked svelte and elegant. She wore a long-sleeved black dress and leather sandals. She had dyed her hair a lighter blue and sported a new hairstyle with wider bangs, cut straight from side to side of her face, which gave her a more Japanese look.

The Trova Latina restaurant was several blocks from the crossing, near a futuristic, round-edged skyscraper, which I vaguely remembered seeing before in some photograph; it was on a side street that looked more residential than commercial. We found the place easily, thanks to Elena's mobile map app; it was the first time she'd been there. Felipe and Lydia had recommended it; they'd eaten there a few times, and according to Elena, knew the owner.

When I came in, I felt a little claustrophobic. It was a small place, not more than ten tables. On three of the walls was a continuous mural of a market in a Caribbean town in a style that reminded me of Diego Rivera.

We were the first customers to arrive. The owner or manager, a middle-aged, tall, ungainly man with a long gray ponytail came to greet us. He welcomed us in Spanish with a faint Caribbean accent I couldn't place.

Felipe's friends? he asked.

Elena nodded and said in English that Lydia and Felipe would arrive soon.

Do you speak Spanish?

I'm afraid not very well, Elena replied.

Is that so? the man asked and gave us a funny smile, as if suspecting we were pulling his leg. Ricardo and Elena?

Elena and I nodded.

I'm César. From Venezuela, he said.

I'm from California, of Mexican origin, Elena ventured, in Spanish.

And you're from Bogotá, César said, looking into my eyes.

I guess Felipe told you.

Cesar nodded. He was going to say something,

but he held back and kept his gaze on mine.

Do you have many Colombian clients?

More or less, he said. You'll see, if you stay awhile.

Do they come late?

Yes, from eleven onward. You're looking for someone, right?

Yes, I replied a little taken aback. Felipe may have told you something…

He said you have a cousin who's gone missing.

Her name is Adriana Torres. She's about thirty, I said and showed him the photo in my mobile phone that mom sent me a few days ago.

I don't think I've ever seen her, César said and rubbed his chin. I'll spread the word, though. Anything to drink? he asked in English.

Two beers, thanks, Elena replied.

Understood, César said and returned to the bar.

What a character, Elena said in a whisper.

Yeah. A bit strange. He reminds me of my uncle, my mother's brother, a sixties or seventies hippie lost in the twenty-first century.

You're horrible, Elena said and took my hands. How did your interviews go?

I think well, I replied. The Japanese lawyer, a man named Tariba, was very kind and said he would help us with whatever we needed. He explained that there's been a recent tax reform in Japan, and two of his clients from whom we need information for the Macau case were just catching up. He asked us to have a little patience, and he promised that he would do everything possible to expedite the procedures. We'll see him again next Monday. The case is complicated because he's counsel to four of the people we're investigating, and he can't give us any information without their approval; it would be against his professional ethics, the lawyer-client privilege.

Is he Ibuke-san's lawyer?

What? Did you talk to Miryam?

Not yet. But in an email that she sent me yesterday, she told me it was one of the questions she was going to ask the lawyer.

It looks that way, I said. The lawyer nodded yes when Miryam asked. He didn't even flinch; maybe he knew beforehand that we were interested in that man. But even with him saying yes, we can't be one hundred percent sure he's the Ibuke-san you're looking for. As you know, until we have all the information, it could just be a simple coincidence.

I know.

What did your detectives find out? I asked.

His parents died ten years ago, and the house where they lived was sold. It is not known who made the sale; the local property register doesn't have that file, or rather they can't find it. The detective in charge said a lawyer could help pressure them to do a thorough search. I've got to talk to Miryam; maybe she can help.

I thought of telling Elena that she should quit the search—maybe Ibuke-san was trouble, as her mother had always told her. If Elena's father was the same Ibuke who was a stockholder in the film studios, he may well be part of the new company involved in human trafficking. This last idea had been shaping in my mind since the meeting with the lawyer. It was a hunch. The man we saw that night in San Francisco, who might have been Ibuke and a client of the lawyer in Yokohama, had gradually become in my mind the samurai Alain Delon represented—that is, a career criminal. Something in his face and his *attitude* that night—the way he acted, how he moved his hands—added to what I now knew of him fed my suspicion.

Did they tell you anything else?

Elena shook her head and patted the table with her right hand, the way she did when she wanted to change the topic. And the diplomats and journalists?

The diplomats were very diplomatic, and the journalists very careful. I felt relieved that Elena didn't want to linger on the topic of her father. I think we intimidated them a little, I went on. My impression was that they were on the defensive, as if we were investigating *them.* They didn't tell us anything that we didn't already know or suspect: the trafficking of women has increased, those responsible are gangsters from both sides, embassies can do little or nothing to prevent it, and the police don't investigate as much as they should.

At that moment Lisa and Veronique arrived. The two wore matching blue Oxford shirts and khaki pants, perhaps they came straight from work where they had to dress like that. Lisa looked a little different; she had cut her hair pixie style. Veronique, on the contrary, looked the same as before, her hair all tangled up, dark smudges around her eyes.

They both hugged me and told me how much they missed me.

We joined another table to ours and ordered more beers. Lisa and Veronique looked genuinely happy to see me and bombarded me with questions: what I thought of Japan, whether I had already taken the law school admission test, what kind of lawyer I wanted to be, whether I liked the job of a paralegal, if I didn't think it too stressful. After a few minutes, I felt a little dizzy; I had not eaten anything other than a noodle soup at lunch. Lydia and Felipe had luckily ordered dinner for everyone, and from one moment to the next the Venezuelan appeared with bowls of rice and plates of fried plantains, black beans, and fried chicken.

Lydia and Felipe arrived when we were about to start eating, and again came the hugs, the toasts to our meeting, and the questions about my future. I felt happier than I'd felt in a long time. During a short break when I didn't have to field any questions and my friends were chatting animatedly, I discreetly took pictures of them with my mobile phone. As I framed their faces on the screen, a wave of nostalgia for times past came over me. I remembered the evening on the terrace of Lisa's house, looking at the bay, when I rejoined the group after an absence of a few months. It was the same night we went to the blues club, and I discovered that Elena interested me much more than I had thought before. It occurred to me that this was happening to me again.

Suddenly a few guitar chords sounded, and the music that was playing at low volume, salsa songs from the seventies and eighties, was drowned out. It was César, and he played a song I knew very well, "Oh, que será" by Chico Buarque, the Brazilian composer, the theme song of a Bruno Barreto movie, *Doña Flor and Her Two Husbands*, which I'd seen a long time ago. César sang it in Spanish, in the original bossa nova rhythm; there are other versions, one in salsa style, by Willie Colón, though with different lyrics. His voice was soft and melancholy, like Buarque's, not at all like his conversational tone, which struck me as abrupt and tense. His demeanor had changed too; he seemed more relaxed and self-assured, on his face a look of contemplation, as if he were praying.

Shortly after the song ended, I turned to Elena and Veronique, who were sitting next to me in a semicircle listening to the song, and hugged them. I told them that I missed them terribly. I couldn't help it; perhaps I was a little drunk. They both laughed and told me it was high time I told them that, and lifted their glasses. I said cheers but I didn't drink any more. I wanted to have all my wits about me when I started asking about Adriana, something I meant to do since we arrived. The place was crowded, and I had heard Colombian accents.

I went to the bar and asked for a glass of water and a hot tea from a waitress who was tending bar while César sang. I asked her if she was Colombian.

Peruvian, she said.

We *are* Colombians, said a tall, stocky young man with a crew cut, who had just come to the bar holding hands with a young woman of medium height and dyed-blond hair.

Have you been in Japan for a long time? I asked.

Several years. Are you a newcomer?

Yes. I'm looking for a cousin of mine.

What's the name? asked the young man.

Adriana Torres.

Adriana Torres, he repeated.

Does she know you're looking for her? the young woman asked in a tone halfway between anger and defiance.

Her family is looking for her, I said, and at that moment I felt somewhat afraid. Everything was happening very quickly; perhaps the couple knew Adriana, and they were protecting her, or it could be the opposite, and she was someone they hated or were after.

And who are you? the young man, asked in the same tone as his girlfriend.

A friend of César's, the Peruvian waitress intervened in a conciliatory tone and pointed with her hand toward the corner where César was standing with his guitar, in his face traces of bewilderment or concern. He had been tuning the guitar for the next song.

Very well, said the young man, and waved to César. Good luck with that search.

I hope you find her, added the young woman and arched her eyes as a farewell.

Before they left, they both looked at me from head to toe, and this time I felt it was an open challenge. I had the sudden feeling that I was in a seedy bar in some forgotten village in the jungle, where differences are squared through fistfights or bullets. The feeling faded instantly. Before me was the waitress, smiling, with the hot tea and the glass of water.

TWO

The next morning, I woke up suddenly. I had just come out of a complicated dream in which I was in a bookstore or library where I'd never been before, looking for a book whose title I couldn't remember, but I knew was an old epic poem I had to read urgently because in it there was a key that would take me back to the place I had come from.

When I opened my eyes, I saw Elena by my side and immediately felt relieved, the dream now a distant memory. Elena was still sleeping; under her eyelids her eyes moved quickly from side to side, a smile on her face. She wore one of my shirts, as she did when she stayed in my apartment in San Francisco; it was a habit of hers that I had not noticed before, but now it made me feel nostalgic for our life as a couple.

It was seven ten by the alarm clock. I noticed I had a message on the answering machine. I got up and went over to the other phone on the desk by the window, where enough daylight came through the half-open curtains.

The message was from José Luis Ramos, the Colombian consul, a tall, dark-skinned man from the Caribbean region, whom we had interviewed the previous afternoon along with his counterparts from Peru, Chile, and Mexico. He said we should call him as soon as we could, that he wanted to give us some additional information. I thought it was odd he said that. He didn't say much during the meeting—he quoted a few statistics, said something brief about loopholes on Japanese immigration law, nothing we didn't know, and seemed impatient; he often looked at his mobile. As soon as we finished, he said that he had an urgent matter to attend to, apologized, and left in a hurry.

Did you sleep well? Elena asked, sitting down on the bed.

Better than I've slept in the last few months, I said.

Another reason you should move to Tokyo.

Someday, why not? But not to this neighborhood.

Our building is in a residential area ten minutes from here, where it's very quiet; you wouldn't know you're downtown.

Is this downtown? From what I've seen there's more than one; the train we took from the airport went through several.

Let's say this is my downtown, the one I know best; I easily get lost in the others. Did you have fun last night?

Of course, I replied and looked her in the eye.

I didn't mean *that.* She stuck out her tongue at me. I meant at the bar.

It was nice at first, but later you couldn't talk, I said. And on the dance floor, if you can call that a dance floor, I got elbowed like a thousand times.

Still, I think you had fun.

I really enjoyed seeing you all.

Like the old days, right?

It's as if time had stood still, I said.

What do you mean?

It's like we haven't been apart for three months.

You're sounding very romantic, Ricardo. I don't know that side of you.

Of course you do, I said, and I threw one of the small cushions of the chair beside me at her with no luck; the cushion fell on the other side of the bed. To my mind came the moment in César's bar when I hugged Elena and Veronique and told them how much I'd missed them. It was something that came over me suddenly and couldn't control.

I saw you went out to talk to César, Elena said and looked absently at herself at the mirror, kitty-corner to the bed. In her reflection, she looked to me more Japanese than when we met at Roppongi crossing; her disheveled hair made her almond-shaped eyes look slightly more slanted.

I was tired of shouting, I said. I saw César going out for a cigarette, and I followed him. I asked about the Colombians I talked to earlier, and he told me that they were not regular customers; they came only occasionally, and he didn't know them well. I had the impression that he knew something else about them but couldn't make up his mind to tell me. What he did tell me was that if he were me, he would be more careful to ask about my cousin; in such cases you couldn't trust anyone, and I would be much better off asking club owners or managers because they usually had a good sense of who is who.

César is right, Elena said. I think you took a risk with that couple. Did you talk about anything else?

Yes, but César is a strange guy, I replied. He talks in riddles. He told me that years ago he had a much larger place, one of the best-known Latino clubs in the city, but that other bar owners in the neighborhood plotted to bring him down, circulating false rumors about people selling drugs in the bathrooms, and other stuff that got him into trouble, and after a few months he had to close it down. Then he changed the subject and talked about Japanese politics, about the right wing, which according to him is everywhere. At some point, he told me that everything was carefully *orchestrated*, and it was amazing how no one noticed. I asked him what he meant by that, and he looked at me in surprise, as if what he'd just said was self-evident and I was pretending not to understand, and he burst out laughing and told me not to pay him any attention; it was an occupational hazard. Then he changed the subject again and returned to the issue of other clubs in the neighborhood, saying that most people in *this scene* know more than they let on but are afraid to talk about it, and there are others who pretend to be blind and say they don't know anything, even if it's happening before their very eyes.

What a strange man, Elena said. What did he mean by *this scene?*

I asked him what he meant, and he told me that in this case it was something like *an underworld.*

Like a criminal underworld?

That's exactly what I asked him. He said it wasn't that precisely, but rather an underworld of people who make a living from nightlife where, according to César, there are all kinds of crooks, from the petty to the most dangerous, including people who are not criminals but somehow outside the law, such as undocumented foreigners, for example.

Elena furrowed her brow. I wouldn't know so much about that; I did hear there's yakuza in this neighborhood, though, she said and got up. She had not buttoned the shirt, which came almost to her knees.

Says who? I asked and went back to bed.

People around here, Elena said casually. People talk about it at work. Felipe also told me, come to think of it. Since his classes have not started, he spends a lot of time with César, who's apparently been in Japan for a long time. I didn't like that guy, to be honest with you, she added. Elena was doing her morning stretching routine as she spoke.

I didn't like him either. I don't think he's a crook, but I wouldn't trust him. The bar is not bad. From seven to eleven it has good vibe, but after midnight it gets a bit seedy.

It looks like you're not used to that *scene*. Elena sat in the chair next to the phone.

I guess so, I said. I've lost a little of my Colombian social smarts living outside the country.

Colombian social smarts?

I mean something like street smarts.

If you really mean to find your cousin, you'll need a lot of that, Elena said and opened the curtains a little wider. From the street came a distant rumor of traffic. The sky was thick with gray clouds.

Our first appointment that day was with Carlos Ozaki, the Japanese-Peruvian editor of a weekly Spanish-language newspaper. According to our original schedule, we should have interviewed him with the consuls and the other journalists, a Spanish and a Chilean affiliated with a Spanish news agency, but he had a last-minute emergency and could not attend.

Ozaki's office didn't have any windows and was lit by noisy buzzing neon lamps. Ozaki seemed to be in a foul mood and didn't agree to let us record the conversation. He said that his newspaper no longer published any local news; they didn't have enough staff, and he didn't know anything specific about the trafficking of women. He had heard of some cases, but nothing more, and he didn't know anyone involved in that sort of thing. Miryam asked him to explain what sort of things he meant, but he turned noncommittal and said that such things were difficult to investigate—no one ever said anything, and it was dangerous. He mentioned a bilingual English-Spanish blog run by someone who signed his name *Ruiseñor* that published articles about the sex trade in Tokyo, including stuff about Latina sex-workers, but he and other journalists he knew didn't know who that person was. After ten or fifteen minutes, Ozaki said he had to leave, and he had already told us everything he knew.

In the afternoon, we took a taxi and went to Saint Xavier's University, where we met with Ramos, the Colombian consul, Naomi Takeyama, the Brazilian sociologist friend of Miryam, and her colleague and companion, Professor Tomás Rodrigues, who turned out to be a Colombian, also from Bogotá. Ramos was the one who suggested they meet all together when Miryam called him before noon. According to the consul, he learned through Takeyama, with whom he'd spoken the night before, that we were going to the university in the afternoon to talk to her and Rodrigues, and he said it was sheer good luck we were planning that because they were trusted friends, and thanks to that we could all meet together at the same time.

The conference room was on the eighth floor of a modern building in the middle of the university campus. It had a large window overlooking a sports area with football fields and baseball diamonds bordered by a railroad track where local trains ran, and beyond, to the city scattered with buildings of various shapes and sizes up to the horizon line. Next to us there was a church, a modern concrete cylindrical structure crowned with a metal cross.

Our research focuses on a Japanese travel agency with offices in Macau, began Miryam after thanking them for coming. We suspect that the Macau branch is where all the trafficking arrangements are made for women of several nationalities to come to Japan to work in the sex industry. What we want to know is if you know women who have come that way.

Several, Ramos said. But, in general, these women don't know anything about the travel agency. The traffickers take care of everything: they arrange for the plane tickets and the visas and deliver them to the women's homes. Their contacts or accomplices meet them at the airport in Tokyo, take away their passports, and give them instructions about their new job; that is, they tell them the truth about the horrible business that they've gotten into. The fact that they deliver their documents to their own homes is important, he emphasized. The traffickers take note of where they live and with whom, and if there are any problems—if the victim refuses to work or wants to return, for example—the traffickers go to their families and threaten them.

Takeyama, who looked a little impatient, nodded several times and tapped her fingers on the table.

I understand your interest in this travel agency in Macau. But what are you planning to do? Professor Rodrigues asked. He was a bald middle-aged man sporting a salt-and-pepper goatee, whose stern features reminded me of my great-grandfather, the one in the photograph at my grandparents' house; he had a somewhat authoritarian yet melancholic air.

That travel agency is one of several companies we are investigating, Miryam said. They are part of a Japanese business group that we suspect has laundered money and evaded taxes in the United States. Apart from Macau, they have investments in Thailand and Singapore.

Thailand and Singapore? Rodrigues interrupted and glanced at Takeyama, as if they had talked about it recently.

That's right, said Miryam. Mostly in the import-export businesses: agricultural products, machinery, and the like.

That complicates things, said Takeyama.

Business groups are very difficult to investigate, Rodrigues added. Naomi and I have been looking at one that has had business dealings in Southeast Asia since the end of WWII. We suspect that some of the principals belonged to a secret society, whose purposes and activities we are yet to find out, but that brought together military officers—and perhaps even war criminals and members of the yakuza. It hasn't been easy, because we only have limited access to the Tokyo and Yokohama chambers of commerce, where the companies of this business group are registered. I'd hoped to find concrete evidence that former war criminals were also involved, but I found nothing conclusive. I did find clear evidence of yakuza involvement, but this is not very damaging because yakuza groups are legally incorporated in this country. A more thorough investigation of their books would be necessary—a forensic accounting, as they say. But for that we need a court order.

I did better in the archives of business and finance newspapers, Rodrigues continued after a pause in which he coughed briefly and drank some of the green tea they had served us. I found some articles that made me think that some of these companies were being investigated by several government agencies. Also by the police, he emphasized. In most cases, for tax evasion. That's always the Achilles' heel of these organizations. It's odd that they have so little common sense; you'd think they would be more careful. In three or four other cases, I found news about lawsuits against them related to scams, embezzlement, and the like. I haven't seen anything to suggest that they were involved with human trafficking, although I'm aware it would be very easy to conceal this aspect of their operations. One of the companies, a subsidiary in Bangkok, brought Thai staff, all women, for a couple of business ventures in Yokohama about fifteen years ago, but from what I've seen everything was done legally.

Rodrigues spoke with a slight Australian accent; the endings of some of his sentences had that sound. His way of speaking, the old-fashioned way he phrased his sentences, reminded me of a professor of Portuguese literature at Berkeley who was, interestingly enough, originally from Australia of Portuguese background. He was one of my favorite instructors, a specialist in Fernando Pessoa, the great Portuguese poet. He spoke very quickly when he lectured, and often, when we analyzed a poem, for example, he would go on long and complicated tangents full of literary references that went from one place to another and generally led to a monologue on theosophy and the Rosicrucian Order, two of his favorite topics.

With the memory of my former teacher in mind, I glanced sideways at Rodrigues and had the odd feeling that he also resembled him, not only in his manner of speaking, but also physically, although the other was younger.

I didn't have much luck either, Takeyama added after a brief silence. While Rodrigues was talking, she had continued drumming her fingers on the table. The only thing I could find, she added, after clearing her throat, is that some of the former employees of the company that Tomás mentioned, were witnesses for the prosecution in the case against the gangster known as Tony, one of the ringleaders of trafficking of Latin American women in Japan, a few years ago. This I found out through one of the volunteers of a community service agency affiliated to Saint Ignatius Church that helps some of the trafficked women escape their *manillas*—that's what they call their handlers who control them; it's the Japanese or Spanish pronunciation of managers. The community service agency is located right next to the church, Takeyama added, pointing. She was sitting facing the window, and those of us on the other side of the table, Miryam, Ramos, and I, turned around to look.

Intriguing, Miryam said, arching her eyebrows. I read several articles about Tony's case, but I didn't know about the witnesses. Why do you think they testified against him? What is the link between the company you were investigating and the Latin American women whom Tony managed?

I really don't know, Takeyama replied. Perhaps they testified against him because of personal animosity or because of some business matter. That company owned one of the restaurants in the area where some of the Latinas worked. Perhaps the fact that the Latinas hung around the very same street caused them problems; costumers might have complained. I can't think of any other reason. I've left that project aside for the time being. Recently, I've been researching the trafficking of Mexican women. I've heard the yakuza are doing business with the northern Mexico cartels these days. Takeyama suddenly stopped and looked at Ramos who looked a little upset. He was texting something on his cell phone.

If I may, Ramos said, looking up, his face slightly flushed. I've got something urgent that may be of interest to all.

We're listening, Miryam said.

A few days ago, a young Colombian woman came to see me at the consulate. She said she wanted to escape her *manilla* and leave the country, not to return to Colombia, but to disappear for a while; that's how she put it. She said she needed a new passport, something that takes time, of course; we have to confirm the identity of the applicant...

Disappear for a while? Miryam repeated.

It's a convoluted case, Ramos said. It's a young woman who was deceived. She was offered a contract as a nurse's aide—same job she had in Colombia—at a private geriatric clinic, in an eastern Tokyo neighborhood. At first, she thought it was a little odd because she didn't have to speak Japanese, only English, but the staff at the Japanese embassy in Bogotá told her everything looked fine, and she accepted.

When she arrived in Tokyo, she was told that the

clinic had unexpectedly closed, and she had to work as a waitress in a Roppongi club—not the kind open to the public, but an exclusive, members-only one. As she had no choice, she accepted. It was an S&M club, and in a matter of three weeks, she decided that she didn't want to do it anymore and ran away. That was two weeks ago. Since then, she's been hiding in the apartment of some Eastern European dancers she ran into by chance when she escaped. She just sent me a text saying the yakuza found out about her whereabouts, and she's now on her way to the embassy…

THREE

I was startled when I heard what Ramos said. Up until then, I'd been listening with interest, but at a certain remove. Although I followed the conversation, to my mind also came varied images of my short stay in Tokyo, especially of Elena wearing my shirt, walking around my hotel room.

I'm sorry to interrupt you, consul, I said. What's the name of the young woman you just mentioned?

Ramos looked at me with keen interest; it was the first time I'd said anything. Miryam had introduced me as her assistant and translator, but beforehand had instructed me to stay out of the conversation, unless somebody needed my help.

It's information I can't share, Ramos replied, and looked at Miryam, who was also waiting to hear what he had to say. Not for the time being, he added. But I think I understand why you ask. Dr. Miryam de Voer wrote to me a couple of weeks ago about the matter with your cousin. Adriana Torres, right?

Yes, I replied.

I can tell you that the woman I'm referring to today is not Adriana Torres; at least I think so, we cannot be sure, people sometimes use other people's identities. In this case, it's a younger woman—as per the documents I have—although they're not always reliable. However, the name rings a bell, he added. It's not in the consulate's current registry; I've already checked. I'd have to look at our past files, something that takes more time. We're a little short on staff now, but I promise I'll take a look myself as soon as I have time, in a couple of days at the most.

Can we all go with you to the consulate? Miryam asked.

If you wish, but I can't guarantee she'll want to talk to you.

If she needs a safe place to stay, we could help her, Takeyama said. It wouldn't be the first time.

The Colombian embassy was housed in a three-story building next to the ambassador's residence, in a quiet and elegant neighborhood of cherry tree-lined streets. We arrived in two taxis, almost at the same time.

The young Colombian woman was in the waiting room, reading a magazine; there was no one else there since the consulate had already closed. She was about twenty-five, slender, of medium height, with light-brown straight hair pulled back in a ponytail. She had a mole on her left cheek.

They are trusted friends, the consul said, and introduced us.

Margarita Rocha, the young woman said and shook hands with us all. She didn't seem anxious or upset. On the contrary, I thought she was glad we were there.

The consul's office was a large rectangular room. On one side, there was a big wooden desk, and on the other, a sitting area with two sofas, one in front of the other, and two leather armchairs. On built-in shelves on the wall, there was a well-stocked library with books and magazines in Japanese, English, and Spanish. Through the only window, in the sitting area, you could see a garden with rosebushes and sculptured hedges, and a small traditional Japanese-style cottage with blue ceramic tiles attached to the Western-style main house.

A middle-aged Japanese woman entered the office after knocking lightly on the door. She brought a teapot and five cups in a tray and left them on the center table.

The passport will be ready the day after tomorrow, said the consul and looked at Margarita. We're only missing the ambassador's signature, who's returning from New York tonight. The fact that you had electronic color copies of all your documents speeded up the paperwork.

Margarita nodded, and said she understood. She was sitting in one of the armchairs diagonal to me, facing Ramos. She wore a gray jacket, a long pleated skirt, white blouse, and medium-heeled shoes. It occurred to me she could pass for a professional woman on a business trip.

The consul told us about your case; we know how you came to Tokyo, and what happened to you, Takeyama said. She was also sitting diagonally across from her, on the sofa she shared with Professor Rodrigues. Her Spanish was fluent, with a faint Portuguese accent. Could you give us more specific details—for example, the names of the people who brought you here and forced you to work at the club?

Everything you say in this office is confidential, added the consul, who looked a little annoyed; perhaps he thought the question was too direct.

I can't give you names because they've threatened my family in Colombia. Margarita said this in a pleading tone, shook her head, and lowered her eyes.

Did you come through Macau? Takeyama asked.

Yes, but we first went to Hong Kong.

Were there other Colombians?

Just me; the other girl was Mexican.

As young as you?

Pretty much, I think. I'm twenty-seven.

The phone rang then. The consul went to his desk and answered. He spoke quickly in Japanese, and looked a little upset. A police officer wants to talk to me; something urgent, apparently, he said when he hung up. I'll meet him in the conference room. I don't know how long I'll be. Don't worry, Margarita, he said and looked at her in the eye. Professor Takeyama and Professor Rodrigues have offered to help you if you need a place to stay tonight. I trust them completely.

Margarita looked from side to side, a little puzzled. I don't know what to do about the visa, she said.

Don't worry, said the consul. I'll take care of that. It'll take a couple of days, though. For now, the most important thing is that you're safe. It would help us a lot if you tell us something about the people who brought you to Tokyo.

Margarita nodded, and looked down.

When the consul left, Miryam, who was sitting next to me, told me in English and in a low voice to ask Margarita what we had agreed in the morning in case we could interview one of the victims.

Like you, I'm from Bogotá, I said, and sat on the edge of the sofa.

Margarita raised her head and smiled halfheartedly.

Our law firm is investigating a Japanese company called Atlas Travel and Tours. Do you know it?

Margarita shrugged slightly and shook her head no.

How long were you in Macau?

One day and two nights, counting the first one; we arrived late.

How many people were waiting for you at the airport?

Two: a man and a woman.

Were they young or old? What nationality?

Chinese, I think. Older, but not that old. The man spoke Spanish, but badly; we almost didn't understand him.

Did they take you to a hotel?

No, we went to a house in the center of the city.

Was it a large elegant house with several rooms?

Yes, large and elegant, but old. It had a moldy smell.

A house like this? Miryam showed her a picture on her mobile phone from the property litigation file. It was a Portuguese colonial house, painted green, with a large balcony on the second floor.

Margarita looked at the photo and nodded several

times.

Are you sure? I asked.

There were pots with begonias on the balcony, she said, and pointed to the photo. The garden fence was also like that, with circular motifs.

Takeyama and Rodrigues, who were sitting in front of us on the other sofa, came to see the photo.

Is that from the case you told me about? Takeyama asked.

Yes, but we're not yet done with it, Miryam replied. Maybe this will help us.

Did you get to know the city? I went on. Miryam wanted as many details as possible.

No, we were very tired. I woke up at noon. The trip was very long. From Bogotá, we went to Madrid, and then to Hong Kong. But we went out to dinner that night. The couple who met us at the airport took us to a restaurant in one of the casinos, on the other side of the city; you have to cross a very long bridge.

Did you meet anyone at the restaurant?

At the restaurant?

Tell us everything, Miryam said. Trust me; it's for your own good.

Two men were waiting for us.

Chinese too?

I think they were both Japanese, but I can't be sure.

Did they tell you anything about your job in Japan?

No, we didn't talk about that. They asked us about our countries: food, customs, things like that. The Mexican girl didn't speak English well, and I had to translate.

While Margarita spoke, Miryam took the personal files from the Macau dossier out of her bag. Each file had stapled pictures of the men.

Was it one of these men? Miryam asked and put the photos on the table, next to the teapot and cups.

Margarita went to the small table and looked closely at the photos, her eyes narrowing. No, she said, none of them, and then returned to her chair.

Right there and then, I was certain that Margarita wasn't telling us the truth, or was hiding something. I noticed her expression had hardened a little when she looked at one of the photos. Miryam had probably noticed the same thing, and looked at her keenly.

Takeyama and Rodrigues, who had also sat on the edge of their sofa and were watching and listening closely, muttered something to each other in Japanese.

Do you know Toro-san? Takeyama asked.

Margarita blushed and shook her head.

Don't lie to us, please. Almost all the victims of trafficking that we've talked to know about him, or know of him through their *manillas*.

Miryam and I looked at each other, baffled.

Toro-san is not in the country, Takeyama said. Don't worry. You know him, don't you?

Margarita nodded and covered her face with her hands.

Is it him you're running away from?

She shook her head no and lowered her gaze.

Who is Toro-san? Miryam asked.

He's a strange character, Takeyama replied. Much is said about him but no one seems to know him in person; he is very slippery. We've been told that he's a sort of investor in this business. Several women I've interviewed told me that it's to him they owe their debt; that is, the money they've been told is the fee for bringing them to Japan. A rumor that goes around says he's also part owner of several nightclubs in Roppongi.

Toro is not a name; it's a nickname, Rodrigues said. It doesn't make much sense in Japanese: it means the fatty part of the tuna, but in Spanish it means bull, which would be an appropriate nickname for someone who inspires fear or has some sort of power.

Interesting, Miryam said and wrote something in her pocket notebook. Is he yakuza?

I don't think so, Takeyama said. We would have known if that was the case. He may have yakuza friends, of course, but I doubt he's a gangster.

Rodrigues served us tea. From the garden came

the hum of an electric pruner. Outside, it was still cloudy, threatening rain.

I thought I should ask Margarita other questions about the couple in Macau; it seemed to me that she had not told us everything, especially about the two men they had dinner with at the casino. What would their role be in all this? But the conversation had taken another turn, and Miryam seemed more interested in this new character, Toro-san, who could be the link that joined the property lawsuit in Macau with the trafficking of women in Japan. If so, there would be more work coming up in the future, more lawsuits, or perhaps other kinds of legal processes I didn't know about. Miryam had said that the Macau lawsuit could be the tip of a giant iceberg, though she had not explained or given examples of what sort of things could be hidden beneath.

I glanced sideways at Margarita; she looked crushed, her nerve and confidence now gone. From the beginning, she'd seemed like an enigma to me: her way of dressing and speaking didn't tell me anything; I couldn't place her. Her accent was from Bogotá, but neutral, perhaps like mine was now after so many years out of Colombia. Maybe she'd also left the country at about the same time; we were about the same age. I could tell by the way she carried herself that she was someone from a middle- or lower-middle-class background; this was an estimate in the style of my father, for whom social class was evident after five minutes of meeting someone for the first time.

Until now, I had not heard her speak English; that would give me other clues because I have a good ear for accents. What struck me the most was the way she shrank at the mention of Toro-san. When Takeyama talked about him, it immediately occurred to me that he might be the man we saw in San Francisco, the samurai, who might be Elena's father and a stockholder of the company we were investigating. Takeyama did not say whether he was young or old, tall or short, slender or heavyset so I could compare it with the portrait I had in my memory. I would have to get more details.

I looked at Miryam, who after her brief exchange with Takeyama had again rummaged through her purse, perhaps looking for another file. I wanted to signal her to ask Margarita, although I could do so myself.

Please understand that we want to help you, Takeyama said suddenly in a soft yet firm tone. Do you owe him money?

Margarita shook her head no again.

We all want to help you, Rodrigues said. But you've got to help us first.

I don't owe Toro-san anything. I've got nothing to do with him.

Tell us, then, who you're running away from, Takeyama urged.

I'm running away from my Colombian *manilla,* Margarita replied, her voice loaded with annoyance. She's the one looking for me. She hired the yakuza who are after me.

FOUR

Margarita agreed to stay in Elena's apartment for a few days, until her papers were in order. The idea came from Miryam who took it upon herself to ask Elena, Lisa, and Veronique—who were luckily all at home when she called, and were happy to help—after ruling out the shelter for battered women in Tokyo that Takeyama and Rodrigues suggested. Ramos told them the yakuza kept a watch on the building and the neighborhood, and Margarita would be in danger the moment she left.

At about seven, Margarita, Miryam, and I arrived in a taxi at the building where Elena lived. Takeyama and Rodrigues took another taxi in the opposite direction; they were going to a lecture at the university and said they would be in touch soon. Ramos stayed at the consulate working on something related to the police visit. He said he had to search for something in the consulate's current registry and added that he would take the chance to look in the older files for my cousin Adriana's registration.

Lisa and Veronique were waiting in their building's reception area. They said that Elena had gone shopping at the pharmacy and would come back soon. The apartment was on the ninth floor and had a spectacular view of the city. The new Skytree Tower, a soaring television tower, was visible in the distance, like a sort of gigantic robot dominating the cityscape from above. The sky was finally free of clouds and a crescent moon was rising over the horizon.

The decor of the living room reminded me of Elena's apartment in San Francisco, though this one was much smaller. There were several low-wattage lamps with colorful shades and the furniture—a large sofa and two armchairs—were upholstered in velvety fabrics. On one of the walls, there was a painting of hers I didn't know, the largest I'd ever seen. It was of a crowd of people waiting to cross a street; the crossing signal was red. The cityscape filled with neon signs reminded me of Roppongi crossing, although everything was blurred.

You'll be safe here, Margarita, Veronique said as we sat down. As you saw, you need a password to get into the building and use the elevator. Most of the people in this floor work at the same school we do, and are easygoing and trustworthy.

Thank you, she said. I truly appreciate your help. It won't be more than three days.

You speak English very well, Lisa said. Where did you learn it?

I lived in New Jersey when I was little. My parents were immigrants, unfortunately undocumented. We went back to Colombia when I was twelve, and I didn't forget it.

You didn't go back to the US?

No. We got deported and couldn't come back for ten years.

It's a pity, Lisa said, and looked at Veronique, who nodded. An awkward silence followed. If you'll excuse us, Veronique said, Lisa and I must prepare dinner. I hope you don't mind eating vegetarian.

Of course not, I said. Margarita and Miryam shook their heads and said thanks.

I know it's not easy to talk about this, Miryam said when Lisa and Veronique went to the kitchen. But it's important that we know as much as possible about your case. It would help us a lot when we start to prosecute them.

Prosecute?

If you don't prosecute them, things will continue as they are. It'll take time, of course.

I don't know what else I can do to help you.

Tell us more about Toro-san. Miryam's tone was urgent but gentle at the same time.

I don't know him well enough; I barely saw him for a few minutes.

How did you meet him? I asked.

In a bar. Toro-san is a very honorable man, Margarita added in a firmer tone. I don't understand why you're so intent in asking about him. He's not the problem. The problem is the people who work for him, and some of his partners.

We already know that, Miryam said. Go on, please.

Before going to work, on an afternoon of my second or third week here, the men who picked me up at the airport took me to a bar. They told me that I was going to meet the person who had helped me come to Japan, and I had to behave well because he was someone very important. I'd resigned myself to my situation by then. I was living with the Mexican girl who came with me—she's a dancer in a striptease joint—and with a Chilean woman, older than us, who worked with me, and who always told me not to worry; she was sure I was going to do well, and she knew what she was talking about, so I should be patient.

I'm sorry, Miryam interrupted. We don't know exactly what kind of work you did; we only know it was an S&M club. Ricardo is my assistant, and he also has to know, she added. But if you're shy about this, you can tell me in private.

No, it's fine, Margarita said and put her hands on her lap. She looked calm, in control of herself. I got the impression she wanted to tell us everything that had happened to her, not because of the value it would have as evidence in court, but because she had to tell someone as a kind of therapy.

I didn't know anything about this, she went on. I'd seen movies, I mean of S&M porno, in Colombia, but it's one thing to watch it and another to do it. Before meeting the clients, the Chilean woman would tell me what the fantasies and the routines were, and how I should behave—that is, what I should do to them or not—and what costumes to wear. We had high school student uniforms, work clothes for nurses and waitresses, and even army uniforms. Apart from that, we had a collection of toys, of course.

The customers were usually middle-aged men, some quite old; they were well dressed, so you could tell they were professionals or people with money. They usually behaved well. They obeyed, of course, because that's the game; although some wouldn't, and sometimes they wanted to go beyond what was agreed and wanted things that made me feel afraid or disgusted.

Did they ever hurt you? Miryam asked.

Never. They didn't touch me, that was a very important rule, but still…

I understand, Miryam said and shook her head slightly. Go back to telling us how you met Toro-san.

The bar was a small dark place, five chairs in the bar and nothing else, all the lights dimmed. Toro-san came in through the back door and sat down beside me where it was darker; I could barely see him. He told me it was a pleasure to meet me; he'd heard good things about me. He sounded polite, spoke English very well, without an accent, as if he were a *gringo*.

I don't know why, but I felt comfortable with him, perhaps because of the way he spoke to me, as if he'd known me from before. I told him they'd tricked me, that I'd had come to work as a nurse's aide. He told me he knew that, and he was truly sorry and I shouldn't take it personally. It was just business, and if I thought about it, the job was not very different from what I would have done in a clinic. I told him I didn't get that. He laughed and told me that in the end, my work was a kind of nursing; men were afflicted by many things that could not be cured by regular medicine and required a different kind of care. I laughed because that was what the

Chilean told me, and now I was beginning to believe it.

After that, he told me that the important thing in that business was *continuity*, and for now, I was the employee, but that in the future, very soon, it was going to be different. I told him again that I didn't understand, and he told me that little by little I would get it; *things would take their shape* in due course.

What things would take their shape? Miryam interrupted.

I don't know. Margarita shrugged. That's what he said, word for word. I imagine he was referring to the business in general: that one day one is the employee and another day one could be the boss.

I know you didn't see him well, but what caught your attention about him? Miryam looked at her watch; it was past eight, so perhaps she was getting impatient.

From the kitchen came the scent of cumin and cardamom.

He was tall and well dressed. When he came in, I saw that he had spiky gray hair, but when he sat down, I couldn't see him well...just his outline. I heard he's an older gentleman, but he sounds younger; his voice is special, like George Clooney's, gentle and masculine. We didn't talk for more than five minutes, and then he said goodbye and shook my hand, as if we had closed a deal. Before leaving, he told me that one of his partners would take care of my debt, so I shouldn't worry, and if I had any problems, he would help me; I only had to give him a call. He left his number on a piece of paper on top of the bar.

Did you ever talk to him on the phone? I asked.

Yes, several times. He would call me to ask how I was doing, if I was getting used to my job, and how I was getting along with his partner, who turned out to be a Colombian woman, a *manilla* we call Cinderella. I'd tell him everything in minute detail. We got along famously on the phone; he's very kind and understanding. When Cinderella started asking me to take on more clients, arguing that I wasn't making her enough money, he told me that he was doing his best to fix the situation, that he needed time and would take care of it himself. That was the last time I talked to him. He didn't call me again. My Chilean roommate said he was out of the country taking care of some important business.

That's when I ran away. I felt unprotected; I thought that Toro-san wasn't coming back, and that any arrangement he made with Cinderella was no longer valid. She's a real bitch; she always wants more and more money. Besides, she's very intense and gets angry easily. She didn't hurt me—physically, I mean—but she'd put me down and humiliate me with her words; she's very cruel.

Tell us about Cinderella, Miryam asked. How did you meet her?

The same night I met Toro-san. She came in when he left, almost at the same time.

Could you describe her?

From her accent, I think she's from Bogotá. I believe she's a little older than me. She uses a lot of makeup; I don't know if I would recognize her without it. She dresses well: brand-name clothes, fine shoes, expensive perfume.

What did she tell you when you met?

That if I behaved well, we would be best friends. Then, she told me how the business was: how much time I would have to work to pay off my debt, how much money I could save afterward, and how much I would need to become *her* partner.

Did she tell you that you could go into the business? Miryam asked. For how much, and how long would it take?

She said that if I counted my pennies, I could be debt free in a couple of years, and I could become partners by the third year.

Miryam was about to ask something else when Elena arrived.

It's good to see you, Miryam said, and she got up and gave her a hug. Let me introduce you to Margarita.

Elena shook Margarita's hand and came to my side to kiss me on the cheek. She was wearing an Oxford shirt and khaki pants, like Lisa and Veronique; it was certainly a kind of uniform.

I don't want to interrupt, Elena said. Please go on, unless it is something confidential, in which case I'll go to the kitchen to see how dinner is going.

It's an informal interview, Miryam said. You can stay if you want. The only rule is that Ricardo and I ask the questions. Ricardo will explain later if there is something you don't understand.

I'll stay then, Elena said and put her backpack on the floor.

Let's go back to Macau, Miryam said. Did you see the people you met at the casino restaurant again?

One of the Japanese guys, the other not.

Tell us.

He was the one that met me at Narita airport and told me about the clinic and the club in Roppongi. I realized then and there that I'd made a mistake, but it was too late. Margarita covered her nose and mouth lightly with her hands, but kept on talking. I realized that I'd been tricked from the beginning. It was so hard to take. You cannot trust anyone! No one, she repeated and put her hands back on her lap.

I don't get it, Miryam said. How was the beginning?

People know what coming to Japan means. People talk. There are many stories—some good, most bad. The good stories used to make me laugh: they were about girls who stayed in Japan for a few years and then came back to Colombia with a lot of money and bought houses, apartments, and taxis; sometimes I believed them, sometimes not, depending on the person telling them; you can tell the liars from afar. I didn't pay too much attention to the bad stories of hard labor and things like that; I thought that you'd have to be very stupid or naïve to fall for it. It never occurred to me that it would happen to me.

On the other hand, I also knew that some people came to Japan to study and work in their professions. A friend of a relative came on a scholarship to study engineering, finished his degree, stayed in Japan, and married a Japanese woman. I don't know him personally, but through him, or rather, through a doctor friend of his, one of my classmates at the university got an offer to work as a nurse's aide at a geriatric clinic in Tokyo.

Was she the one who recommended you for the job?

Yes, it was her. She wrote me letters, called me on the phone. See Margarita, you're going to make a lot of money here; the job pays very well, and you speak better

English than I do; I swear to you you're going to do very well.

I would ask her what you had to do, and she said that it was like the internships we did at school at the clinics. She said that it wasn't particularly difficult—they were all quite old and affectionate, and especially very generous if you did your work well. Everything was a lie; she worked, but in *this* business. I didn't know, of course; I didn't even suspect. I fell for it; I believed everything. We were classmates and friends…

FIVE

After dinner, Miryam, Elena, and I went to César's bar. Miryam said that she had been intrigued by what we had told her about the place and wanted to see it with her own eyes. Lisa and Veronique stayed at home, chatting with Margarita, who seemed relieved and comfortable in the company of my friends.

On the way, Miryam asked us what we thought of Margarita. Elena said that she liked her; she seemed trustworthy, although it was hard for her to understand why she had been so easily deceived. I only said that it must have been very difficult for her to face that sort of situation, that anyone else would be traumatized. I was still convinced that Margarita had lied to us in the afternoon when Miryam showed her the photos of the men in the Macau file, and that bothered me. I understood that she could not betray the traffickers for fear of what they could do to her family in Colombia, but there was something about her—her demeanor, her attitude—that did not fit and made me doubt her. Miryam looked at me a little incredulously for a moment; perhaps she also had her doubts about Margarita's honesty and said it was a stroke of luck that we met her, and if we did things right, she would lead us to the head of the organization.

When we were about to enter the bar, two young guys and a girl hurried out. The first one to come out, broad-shouldered and of Japanese descent, almost bumped into me; we looked at each other dumbfounded, for an instant. The other one, tall and short-haired, had a cell phone in his hand, and said, we are already on the way, please wait; his girlfriend, a young woman of medium height and wavy dyed-blond hair seemed distressed and said let's run, or we won't ever see her again.

Miryam asked me if I knew what had happened and I repeated what I heard in English, and said that I would ask César later. Only after a few seconds did I realize that the couple who came out were the Colombians with whom I had spoken the other night.

We sat at the only free table, near the door. The place was crowded, and people were chatting loudly. There was a fragrance of coconut in the air, which suddenly reminded me of my grandparents' house in the mornings, when my grandmother was doing her prayers. Instinctively, I looked to the floor, next to the wall, and found the bamboo receptacle where the aroma came from.

Most of the tables were occupied by Latin Americans, some of them of Japanese descent. César was with three couples who had joined two tables next to the bar. They were older, about his age, maybe close friends. One of the women wore a birthday hat and looked very animated. She wore a tight red dress and had a lot of makeup on her face.

The Peruvian girl who tended to the bar came to our table and told us that we could still order food because the kitchen was going to be open until dawn. It's a special night, she added. We're celebrating our third anniversary, and the birthday of one of our clients. You were lucky to find a free table.

Welcome, said César, who came behind the waitress. He wore a white linen *guayabera* with gold-colored embroidery that gave him the air of a master of ceremonies. The first round is on the house, he said in English and looked at Miryam.

Thank you, said Miryam and introduced herself.

The pleasure is mine. César made a small bow. You've probably heard that it's a special night. We'll have a musical show in a few minutes, a couple of singers of *rancheras* and *boleros.* We're going to get a little sentimental, I hope you don't mind. To remember is to live again, as that wonderful song goes. As he said that, he looked keenly at Miryam; perhaps he found her attractive, or she looked like someone he knew. He was about to say something, but he changed his mind; he made another short bow, this time a little stiffly, and said to please feel like at home.

Would you have a minute? I asked as he was leaving.

César smiled formally. Let's take some fresh air.

Out in the street, the traffic was heavy but moving swiftly.

I love the energy of this city, I said.

César cleared his throat and looked at his wristwatch.

I apologize for interrupting you this way, I said.

Don't worry. I understand you're worried about your cousin. I asked around, but I didn't find out anything. Now that the weekend has started, there'll be more people to ask. But let me do the talking, OK?

Thanks a lot, I said.

Sure. No problem, my friend.

The Colombians who left a while ago were in a big hurry, I said.

Everybody's in a hurry in Tokyo, César said and looked in the direction of Roppongi crossing, four or five blocks away, from where flashes of neon signs and giant television screens came. They were probably going to another party, he added. There are many Latin clubs in this neighborhood. It's party time, as your people say.

Places like yours?

Pretty much, but bigger; some with enough floor space for dance classes, which are very good business; these days all Japanese want to dance salsa or merengue, and also tango. César said this in a flat, monotonous tone and looked up at the sky, where there were thick white clouds with gray edges, the waxing moon hidden behind them. He looked tired; I noticed that his eyes were a little bloodshot. He took out of his pocket a pack of cigarettes and offered me one.

I shook my head and asked who the birthday woman was.

A great friend, he said. She is a Cuban who's been in Japan for many years; she's married to a Japanese lawyer who specializes in immigration law and works with him. She has helped many people with the paperwork for permanent residence or gets them out of trouble; sometimes people behave badly, as if they were back in their country. She writes a column about life in Japan in one of the Latino weekly papers.

I didn't know there were weeklies in Spanish.

Mostly online, but some also come out in print. We have some at the bar, if you're interested.

Speaking of journalists, do you know Javier Pinto?

César arched his eyebrows and slapped me on the shoulder. Don't tell me your girlfriend works at the language school two blocks from the crossing.

Yep.

Of course, of course, he said. That's why you know about Javier. He occasionally works for that school, which has branches everywhere. It's a great business, you know.

Is he the one they call Ruiseñor?

César laughed. It's a badly guarded secret, he said. Those who know him know it. But you're not going anywhere with what Javier writes, he added. He's a friend of mine, and I love him, but he lives in another world, in another galaxy. He was a partner in this business for a while, by the way; but he's not a man made for this life. If you want, I'll give you his phone number, although I think he's traveling somewhere in Asia. He's always traveling.

Do you mean that the articles he writes are not reliable?

I don't mean that at all, César said, and frowned. The thing is that Javier writes for an audience that *knows* nothing at all.

How's that?

He writes for people who don't know this scene; I mean, for the general public. From time to time, he publishes in one of the English newspapers, for an audience that is even more naïve. In this country information is good business; there are thousands of newspapers and magazines, not to mention the Internet. There is information about everything you could want. But when it comes to in-depth reporting, they come up a bit short; there are many taboos and even more self-censorship, and what gets published is seldom worth the paper it's printed on. Javier is quite good, though. I mean, he writes well, but his stuff is not journalism, at least not committed journalism, as done in other places and other times. I think he's more into fiction. If I'm not mistaken, he's writing a novel about postwar Japan or something like that.

Have you known him for a long time?

Yes, a long time. From our days in Bangkok, many years ago—so many that I no longer remember—when Bangkok was interesting, not the city it's now.

Do you think he knows Adriana?

Maybe, but I doubt he knows her well. Javier looks at things from afar. He knows many people, but he doesn't have many friends. He's a bit reserved, especially with women. If Adriana is someone who has told him things for his articles, I doubt they are friends. He takes care of himself and doesn't get mixed-up with anyone.

What do you mean?

I mean, Javier doesn't like to mix business with pleasure.

Ah, yes, I understand.

You understand, but you don't understand, right? I think you're a little *gringo*, like Javier.

Gringo?

It's a joke. Your friends are probably on their second drink. Let me give you Javier's phone number and email. If you find him, tell him that you talked to me, he added, handing me a business card he took out of his wallet.

When we came back in, César went directly to the small stage next to the bar and introduced the performers who turned out to be one of the couples who had been at the birthday table. The man wore a Mexican mariachi suit, and the woman, a colorful yellow dress. They both had guitars that they briefly tuned.

They started in a duet with "Para Morir Iguales," a well-known ranchera about a search for lost love. They made a fine duo; their voices were deep and well tempered. No doubt they were professionals. When they reached the chorus, some of the customers sang with them. *Te buscaré por cielos y por mares, rompiendo mi destino, para morir iguales.*

After a big round of applause, they sang other rancheras and some old-fashioned boleros about heartbreak and despair, as if the reason of the party was not a birthday celebration or an anniversary, but rather mourning or the commemoration of a tragic event. For some of the songs, the mariachi added a soundtrack—trumpets, violins, and bass—with a karaoke machine placed down at his feet.

Miryam and Elena looked very entertained by the show. From time to time, they would say something to each other in a whisper and smile. The other customers listened quietly or hummed softly. César served shots of tequila behind the bar that the Peruvian waitress took to some of the tables, perhaps to those of loyal customers or his friends. Those who received them toasted in silence with the performers and with César, who watched attentively in all directions, perhaps to make sure that he did not forget anyone.

It occurred to me that César was a sentimental man with a complicated past; perhaps he was divorced and had children, or a history of failed relationships. I was surprised to hear that he knew Javier Pinto from years ago. I couldn't imagine them as friends. They didn't seem to have anything in common, although I didn't yet know Javier; I just had a general picture of him through my friends. That they'd met in Bangkok also seemed odd. It was not, as far as I knew, a destination for Latino immigrants; I couldn't imagine what had brought them there.

After about half an hour or so, the mariachi said they would take a break, and would come back later. His partner bowed several times, and all the lights went back on. People applauded loudly, and some stood up; they looked truly moved.

César picked up the microphone and told the audience to remember that breakfast began at five o'clock, and as usual, they would close the front door and keep the back door open.

Some couples stood up and went to the bar to pay the bill; others went out into the street; maybe they had already paid or would be back soon. Several tables near us were now empty.

Elena and Miryam were surprised that the evening performance was over so soon. I told them that maybe people would go dancing to one of the nearby clubs and would return at dawn to have breakfast.

Miryam asked me where the singers were from, and I told her I didn't know—probably they were South Americans, maybe Colombians or Ecuadorians, or even Peruvians, that I would have to ask.

They're not Mexicans? Elena asked, a little surprised.

They're Ecuadorians, César said, who arrived at our table with a bottle of tequila and four shot glasses.

From Guayaquil. Do you mind if I join you for a moment? May I pour? It's on the house.

Of course, thank you, Miryam said.

So, you're all looking for Adriana Torres?

In some way or another, Miryam said.

Now I remember who you are, César went on, while pouring the liquor. At first, I wasn't sure; but now, thanks to the music, I'm sure. I never forget a face.

Did we meet somewhere? Miryam asked.

No, I didn't have the pleasure. You're friends with Naomi Takeyama, the Brazilian professor, right? You went to have a drink at my old bar, near Roppongi crossing. That would be about two years ago, if I'm not mistaken.

You've got a great memory, Miryam said.

That changes everything, César said in a serious tone. I owe a debt of gratitude to Naomi, and that's why I'm going to tell you what I know. I don't think I can help you much, though.

Any information you have would be great, I said.

The Adriana Torres from the photo you showed me the other night is someone who doesn't want to be found, much less rescued, César said.

How's that?

As simple as that. She doesn't want to be helped.

Why not? I asked.

Because things are more complicated than they seem. Right now, she isn't anyone's victim. Or rather, let's say she's a victim, but of her own greed. Having said that César took a swig of his drink.

I don't understand what you mean, Miryam said.

Neither do I, Elena added.

I didn't say anything but felt a kind of uneasiness, as if about to hear bad news.

Adriana Torres is a *manilla*; someone who has women who work for her, César said in a low voice and gestured to us to draw closer to him. Do you know what I mean?

We all nodded.

She came five or six years ago, as many do; that is, deceived, he said in a low voice. She had it rough. She worked in a third-rate club in Kabukicho, a seedy part of town; after that she worked as an exotic dancer at a club, I think. Naomi helped her back then, but it didn't work out. She went into hiding, I'm not sure where, in a battered women's shelter, I think, but the yakuza found out and pulled her out. After that, they sold her to another trafficker, an important guy. This changed her life completely, because he's one of the big fish, and he's supposed to be an honorable man.

Honorable man? Elena asked in a tone loaded with irony.

From what I've heard, he's an understanding boss, who treats his employees or people who *owe* him money well. Someone told me that he was well educated, and a bit old-fashioned when it comes to giving his word and things like that. Don't ask me how to find him because I don't know. The only thing I can tell you —because it just came to me— is that his nickname is Toro-san.

The guy Naomi mentioned, Miryam said as to herself.

Elena looked at her in surprise.

I'll tell you later, Miryam said.

Naomi should know about him, César ventured. I doubt she knows him personally, though. Javier Pinto also knows about him, he said a bit louder and looked at me, as if I had suddenly made him remember something important. Yes, yes, he went on, and scratched his head. This was a few years ago. Javier told me that he was the *man behind the scenes, who pulled the strings from afar.* Apparently, he only comes to Japan a couple of times a year. If I'm not mistaken, Javier said he was based in Thailand…

SIX

On Sunday afternoon Elena and I went by metro to the Meiji Shrine Park. Miryam had an emergency meeting with the rest of our team, who had been inquiring about the companies Tariba was a proxy for at the chamber of commerce. She said that I could take the day off, and we would talk about work in the hotel in the evening.

The subway car was almost full, and we had to stand. Some of the service windows were open, and the shrieking of the metal wheels on the rails got on my nerves, and I had to close my eyes to relax. I felt a little dizzy. I had not slept well. I had spent the night tossing and turning in bed. I couldn't stop thinking about what César had said about my cousin Adriana, which at first seemed to me a perverse fabrication. Hard as I tried, I couldn't imagine her in the role of perpetrator. My image of her was still that of the teenager I was once in love with: slender, cinnamon-skinned, and cheerful and vivacious, though also naive: she laughed at anything new that she didn't know, as if she was truly astonished that the world was so diverse. I remembered the end-of-the-year party when she told me she wanted to travel and see the world. How could she have gotten mixed up in this?

What really kept me up, though, was the thought of my mom and Adriana's mom reaction when they learned about the kind of work she did and why she wasn't going back to Colombia. Mom was too sensitive and would take it very hard. She wouldn't talk about it; she wouldn't share it with anyone, especially with Dad. I didn't know Sofía, Adriana's mother, well; all I remembered of her was that she was a generous and cheerful woman who was always a little loud when she talked, but I imagined that the news would crush her. Mom told me that since Sofía had been widowed, Adriana had become the center of her life.

Are you still thinking about your cousin? Elena asked when we left the station. The day was sunny, but across the sky were several banks of dark clouds, threatening rain.

I can't help it. The news killed me.

I hear you. Are you going to call your family? You can use my phone if you want.

I'll call when I'm back in San Francisco. It's going to be a difficult conversation. I hope Dad doesn't hear about it.

I feel bad for you.

What would you do in my place?

I don't know. My family is not like yours. Well, it's very small—it's Mom and me. Although, now that you mention it, there's you, and Lisa, and Veronique.

Are Lisa and Veronique your family?

We've been *sisters* ever since we met, but now I feel like we're real sisters.

I was surprised that Elena said that about Lisa and Veronique. I'd always thought Elena was a little averse to that sort of closeness. She had always been very affectionate with everyone in the group, though at the same time, she kept her distance. I had not imagined that sharing a living space would change that; in fact, I'd imagined the opposite: one day she would grow tired of so much closeness and would decide to live alone, in her own place, even if it was a tiny studio apartment. But perhaps I was judging her from my own tainted perspective. My brother and I had never gotten along, and if it weren't for our family bond, I wouldn't have anything to do with him at all.

I truly admire you, I said.

Don't be silly. They're both very sweet.

You think Veronique is sweet?

As I told you before, I'll never understand what

happened between you two. With me she's a very different person from what you've told me.

By the way, did you call them this morning?

First thing in the morning, when you finally fell asleep. Don't think I didn't notice you couldn't sleep. Lisa told me that the consul had called in the evening to tell Margarita that all her documents would be ready by Monday afternoon.

And what did Margarita say?

It seems she's was very happy. From what Lisa told about how they spent the evening, I got the impression that the three of them got along famously.

If you don't watch it, they'll add you another sister, I said.

What happened to Margarita is awful, Ricardo. I can't imagine the nightmare she must have gone through. I also understand your cousin's case, although it's more complicated.

They're quite different.

That may be so. But if you're poor, and they con you, and you're out of options…

My cousin wasn't that poor.

So she had the same chances you had? Berkeley and all that?

You're right, Elena. It's just that I'm mad at her. I don't understand why she did that.

Well, maybe you don't really know her.

You're right. I don't really know her.

Let's change the subject, shall we? Elena took my hand and pulled me forward. We'd stopped at the pedestrian crossing, and the light had changed to green.

We walked in silence for a few minutes. The park was a forest of tall, leafy trees, among which ran a soft breeze that smelled of damp earth.

Did I tell you that I'm taking a Japanese calligraphy class with a well-known artist? Elena asked.

You didn't tell me.

Ogawa, my boss, recommended me to her. She's a bit eccentric and puts too much makeup on her face, like a geisha. She also calls me Rita-san; Ogawa probably told her to. In any case, she's very talented; she also does woodblock printing in traditional Japanese nineteenth-century style.

Is it at a school? I asked.

No, the class is at the headquarters of an old artists' society, near another park, in Ueno, on the other side of town.

Does your teacher have more students?

I think several; some are foreigners. She only teaches those who have a genuine interest in Japanese aesthetics. She took me in because I came highly recommended by my boss, as I told you. It is a rather exclusive society in that sense.

Genuine interest?

Yes, *genuine* interest, Elena repeated and looked at me with a grimace of mock reproach.

Is it a secret society?

Not at all, Ricardo. Why are you asking me that?

Sorry. Sometimes I can't get things off my mind. When you said that it was a rather exclusive society I remembered that Professor Rodrigues mentioned a secret society during our meeting…

Well, the one thing has nothing to do with the other. Mine is about the arts, yours is about business.

Elena stopped abruptly on the gravel road where we were walking and pointed ahead, toward a large Shinto gate made of concrete.

It's the entrance to the sanctuary, she said. It's a very important one, you know. It's dedicated to the spirit of Emperor Meiji, who expedited the modernization of Japan.

I read something about it in my *Lonely Planet* book, I said.

We went around the sanctuary square, where there were two large bushy trees, and went to the main enclosure, a wooden structure with an imposing green roof that glowed when the sun touched it. I kept busy taking pictures with my cell phone while Elena made a quick pencil sketch of the building.

When we finished our visit and were heading back to the subway station, Elena looked worried; her brow was slightly furrowed.

What are you thinking about?

Many things, Elena replied and sat on a bench beside the sidewalk. Like you, my head is spinning. I suddenly thought of mom. Last night, I couldn't get her out of my head.

Courtesy of the Ecuadorian mariachis, I said and sat down next to her.

I thought about that, too. I'm embarrassed, especially with you, that I don't know much about Latin America, even Mexico. Mom hardly ever talked about her life in her country when I was little. In fact, I was surprised when one day she told me she was born there. She told me that I didn't have to care about it. I was an *American* girl, and the rest was *nonsense.* I asked her why and she got angry; she told me to stop messing around. I told you several times that Mom drove me nuts with her riddles, so I left that on the side. I found out things on my own. I had a classmate at school who was also of Mexican origin, and she told me about her relationship with her mother, which I realized was worse than mine because it was the other way around: she demanded that she speak Spanish at home, go with her to Catholic

Mass, and to visit friends and relatives, where my friend was bored out of her mind. We became close; we were rebels, or so we believed. She told me that I was lucky because I didn't look Mexican; or rather, that people didn't take me for Mexican or Chicana, which was often the case with her.

How did you feel?

I don't know. On the one hand, I thought I was lucky people didn't take me for Mexican or Chicana; not because I understood what it was all about, but rather because people left me alone; they didn't call me names or make stupid comments, as they did to my classmate. I was not very friendly at the time, though, and kept people at a distance. I was a tough cookie, as you like to say. Things changed a few years later, when a new girl came to our class, who was Japanese-American from both sides. We became fast friends; she was also shy. Unfortunately, our friendship didn't last long. One day when we were talking at lunchtime, I told her that my father was Japanese, and she took a long look at me and said that it was a lie; it couldn't be, because there was nothing Japanese about me. That was the last time we talked; I hated her from that day forward.

How old were you?

Eleven or twelve, I don't remember; but I started to cry. I took it hard, it depressed me, and I couldn't keep it in. They called my homeroom teacher and one of the school counselors to calm me down. Mom was furious, of course. She'd always told me not to say anything about my father, and, that if someone asked me, I should say that he was Italian from Rome and had died when I was a child. Can you believe it? I told you my mom hardly ever mentioned my father, though she kept that picture, the one where he's dressed in mariachi style; the one I ruined. Last night when we were at the bar, it occurred to me that my father was there. I know it doesn't sound very rational, but I thought so. I even looked carefully at all the tables, hoping that I would see him there. Did you see that during the performance some Japanese men came in?

I didn't notice. Wouldn't they be Latin Americans of Japanese origin?

I don't think so. They wore *sarariman* business suits.

So, Latinos here can't be businessmen?

You're right. Maybe they were Latinos. They were there only for a few minutes. They looked around and left. They were young, not of my father's generation, so I didn't pay much attention to them.

SEVEN

Tariba, the lawyer, called Miryam in the morning while we were preparing for the meeting, to suggest that instead of having it at the hotel's business center as we had agreed, we hold it at a corporate boardroom that his firm had at its disposal in a building nearby us; he said he would send one of his staff to pick us up at the hotel lobby. Miryam kindly accepted, but when she hung up, she said that the sudden change of venue made her think that Tariba was up to something.

It looks to me like Tariba will bring reinforcements this time. I'm pretty sure he is aware that our young Japanese colleague has been requesting information about his clients' businesses at the chamber of commerce.

What do you think he's planning? I asked.

I don't know, but I have a bad feeling about this. Tariba is an experienced lawyer who specializes in high-stakes commercial disputes and litigation in several jurisdictions. For the time being, we have to make sure he doesn't push us into a corner or force us to make decisions that we'll have to regret in the future. I'd like you to pay careful attention to what he says and does and tell me what you think afterward.

All right, I said. I'll watch him carefully. During our first meeting, I got the impression that he knew exactly what we were going to ask him, as if he had already rehearsed our meeting in his mind.

Yep, I also noticed that, Miryam remarked. Tariba is an old fox. He knows his weak points and defends himself well. With him, you've got to have a well-crafted plan or surprise him with something unexpected.

The conference room was on the eleventh and top floor of a modern building at Roppongi crossing, which we reached by a private elevator. It was a large and elegant room, with a zelkova table for twelve people and a large window overlooking the street. Hanging on one of the side walls, was a Japanese calligraphic triptych on parchment paper that looked like an antique, and at the other end, under a large flat-screen monitor, an Ikebana floral arrangement in a ceramic *raku* vase.

Tariba greeted us warmly, as if we were old friends that had not seen each other in a long time. He apologized for the change of venue and assured us that we would be more comfortable here and would not have to worry about anything as we had everything we needed at hand. When it was my turn to shake his hand, I noticed that today he was a little stooped. Tariba was a slender man, taller than me, as tall as my brother, though today he looked a bit shrunken; perhaps he had arthritis or some sort of bone deficiency.

Sit down please, he said, pointing to the side of the table facing the window. Two men and one woman, smartly dressed like Tariba, entered the room. Tariba introduced them as his team of advisers. The two men said they specialized in tax law, and the woman, in international law. Each had several folders of documents, and a laptop. After the introductions where we exchanged business cards, Tariba took the floor.

There are some new points we have to discuss, he said, in a somewhat ceremonial tone.

Miryam nodded her head.

At our first meeting, Tariba began, I mentioned that the finance ministry has recently introduced new tax regulations that affect Japanese companies that have subsidiaries or branches in other countries. Well, we've been closely studying the impact of these new laws on our pending litigation in Macau. It hasn't been an easy task because this new tax reform has several provisions that can be interpreted in numerous ways, and we had to consult with officials in the ministry to understand their full scope. Tariba paused and looked at us over the lenses of his spectacles, perhaps to ensure that we were following his thread. Today, he spoke in a way that seemed different from the first time, though perhaps I had not paid much attention then. He suppressed or extended the endings of some words, which gave him sort of a Boston accent. For a moment, I had the crazy idea that he was another man, a doppelgänger, not the man with whom we had spoken just a week ago.

We've noticed, Tariba continued with some urgency, that in addition to an increase in the tax rate payable to the Japanese treasury, there are new regulations regarding the handling of legal disputes that arise with foreign parties, as is the case that concerns us. Tariba stopped, but this time he looked at his colleagues, who immediately nodded.

I have copies of a certified translation of the tax reform documents that concern us, he said, and looked at the young lawyer who handed us the documents. If you have any doubts about the text, my colleague can help you, he said. Certified translators sometimes use archaic words or unnecessarily make a mess of what is obvious.

Miryam leafed through the documents and motioned to me to do the same. There were thirty double-spaced pages, plus an additional three-page glossary.

As you can see on page 10, Tariba continued, indicating that we should follow him in the text, the ministry requires that foreign parties should engage competent local professionals—that is, lawyers who are experts in tax legislation and registered in our country. It goes on to say that this is common practice in other developed countries.

Miryam read the page thoroughly and made some notes in her notebook. I understand, she said. We'll have to get fully acquainted with the new regulations. It is clear to me that the new requirements will delay the process, but I doubt it will affect us otherwise.

Take as long as you need, Tariba said. In the meantime, I would like to add something to the background. We have further documentation that we have just obtained in Macau, which shows that the second property in question, the small house attached to the main house, was leased from 1948 onward to several tenants, some of whom—without our clients' knowledge—used that residential space for commercial activities. Let us remember—no evidence has yet been presented to indicate that such commercial activities were illegal, and the local police never received any complaints worth noting. We understand, of course, that there is the possibility of collusion or complicity with the Portuguese authorities, especially between the postwar period and the transfer of sovereignty to China in 1999. Tariba paused again and put his hands in the pockets of his vest; he had them resting on the table, on either side of his file folders. My young colleague will give you copies of the documentation I just mentioned, he added.

The young lawyer hurriedly gave us the documents.

I thank you for your explanation and diligence, Tariba-san, Miryam said. I'm aware that this requires additional work. Perhaps we could move on to another topic that might help us speed things up.

Speed things up? Tariba rubbed his chin. I don't understand what you mean.

It's about Ibuke-san, whom I mentioned at our first meeting. It's a delicate matter. I understand that he was also a shareholder of a film production company, when he lived, or rather, when he temporarily resided in Los Angeles.

Yes, of course, Tariba said and moved around the papers before him; he seemed to be looking for something, or perhaps he just wanted to make time to think what to say. Ibuke-san is an old client, he added after a few seconds while he put each page in the order he wanted. The company that you mentioned was dissolved long ago and everything was done legally, within the scope of the laws at the time; I took care of it myself. Regarding his temporary stay in the United States, he had a work permit that we obtained so he could freely come in and out of the country…

What we're interested in is personal: a family matter, actually, in the early 1980s, Miryam interrupted.

I see. Tariba drummed his fingers on the table. Something unexpected; I had not imagined it would be about that.

Just then, a young woman dressed in a sky-blue uniform brought tea. While the woman served, Tariba chatted quietly with the young woman lawyer, who was sitting to his left. He looked agitated, his face flushed, but maybe it was normal for him. Elena said Japanese people blushed easily.

Miryam, on the other hand, was the picture of calm. She read the document that Tariba gave us, and there was nothing on her face that betrayed what she felt as she went through it, quite the opposite to her usual demeanor at the office, where her face had a more varied range of expressions when working on a case. Perhaps it was the bearing she adopted for litigation, at the courts, or with opposing legal counsel. Whatever it was, Miryam clearly had the advantage right now in terms of strategy.

I think we're on the right track, Miryam said in a low voice, in Spanish.

Aren't you worried about the new legislation? I asked.

I expected it, she whispered in English.

Tell us exactly how we can help you, Miryam-san, said Tariba once the young woman who served us tea left.

For now, we would like to know about Ibuke-san's properties in the United States. I understand he owns several houses and condominiums in California.

I am not authorized to say anything concerning Ibuke-san's properties. But tell me one thing: Is anyone making any claims against Ibuke-san in the United States?

I'm not allowed to say anything about it.

I see. Tariba feigned a smile.

Tariba-san, the only thing I can tell you right now is that it's in everybody's best interest to put all our cards on the table. I could call my client right now and request permission to discuss the matter with you. It's a good time to call, given the time difference. I can't assure you that I can get through, but I'll try.

A very reasonable proposal, Miryam-san; you may use the first office to the right of the elevator, the telephone is by the window. In the meantime, we'll take a brief recess.

Tariba said he would be back in a few minutes, that he also had to make a call. When he left, the young lawyers' faces relaxed, and they began to talk animatedly.

I got up and went to the window. The day had started with clear skies, but now there was a layer of bulging clouds that veiled the sunlight. On the sidewalk, at the intersection across from us, I noticed a woman wearing high-heeled shoes coming out of a taxi parked by the curb with its hazard lights on. She wore a raincoat, and on her head, a bright-colored scarf, or perhaps a turban. When she got on the sidewalk, she looked up in our direction, her two hands on her forehead as a visor. When she lowered her arms, though, she staggered and fell; perhaps one of the heels had broken. The woman remained motionless for a moment without anybody noticing, and after a few seconds, she struggled and got up by herself. One of the heels had indeed broken, and she now limped.

One of the young lawyers, who had also been standing and looking out of the window, though probably in another direction, came to my side and asked me if I had been a long time with the firm. His question took me by surprise; I didn't know whether he knew I was only a paralegal. I told him that just for a few months, still undergoing training.

I'm interested in the calligraphy painting, I said to change the subject and turned to look at the wall. What is it about?

Ah, it's a philosophical theme, he said, and crossed

his arms. The characters express key concepts in Japanese aesthetics: seduction, pride, and renunciation. They were formulated by a famous Japanese philosopher of the 1930s. If I am not mistaken, they have been the subject of great controversy in academic circles. I really don't know much about it. What I can tell you is that it's an original work by an artist of the time. One of the founders of the firm inherited it from his father, who had a very important collection that is now in a well-known museum.

You speak English very well, I said.

Not as well as I'd wish, the young man said, and waved his hand several times, as if in a negative. I took an intensive legal English course for lawyers in San Francisco for six months last year. During that time, I was also part of a team in charge of a corporate event organized by the Japanese consulate and the San Francisco Chamber of Commerce to promote business exchanges. Thanks to that, I had the opportunity to make several American friends who helped me with my pronunciation.

Was it at the Nikko Hotel?

Precisely. Did you attend?

No. I knew about it; perhaps I read something about it in a newspaper.

Of course, of course. We advertised in the papers.

The young man was about to say something else, but Miryam and Tariba had just returned. It was a pleasure to talk to you, he said and gave me a half bow and went back to his seat, to the right of Tariba.

Let's continue with our meeting, dear friends, Tariba said, his face more relaxed than before. You have the floor, Miryam-san.

My client claims to be Ibuke-san's daughter. She was born in Los Angeles in 1977. Her mother of Mexican origin, now a US citizen, married Hiroki Ibuke in November 1976. I don't have copies of the documents right now, but it would be a matter of one or two days. Once paternity is proved, my client would begin the process of acquiring Japanese citizenship and would probably move to Japan permanently.

Unfortunately, that will not be possible, Miryam-san. Ibuke-san will not recognize paternity. He has given me very precise instructions about that. Furthermore, for your information, there is no law that requires a Japanese citizen to undergo a DNA test. Japanese nationality law is a bit more complex than it is in your country. In cases related to paternity, for example, it is not enough to establish a genetic relationship; you also must prove that there was or is a bond.

Thank you for reminding me of that, Tariba-san. The claim we have in mind would be made in the United

States, where family laws are different and tend to favor the affected party. Keep in mind that Ibuke-san abandoned his lawful wife and daughter.

Your client is entitled to do so, but you know that's not going to solve anything.

Unless Ibuke-san is forced to return to the United States.

What do you mean?

We are filing a lawsuit in a San Francisco court against Ibuke-san later this month. As I said before, it's time to put all our cards on the table.

EIGHT

When Elena and I went out to eat, the sky was completely overcast, and there was a blistering breeze. César was alone in the restaurant; he said he had just arrived and sat down with us to talk.

He began by telling us how he'd left Venezuela in the late 1980s, at a time when his family had gone bankrupt and the local currency, the bolivar, had crashed. He said that he traveled around Europe, mainly in the east, where he made several friends playing music, and after months of moving around working as a musician in bars and clubs, he fell in love with a Dutch woman and ended up living with her for a couple of years in Australia. After that relationship crumbled, he went on a long trip through South East Asia; and in Bangkok, he met a Japanese businessman who hired him as a musician and salsa teacher for a little club in Tokyo, where he worked for several years, before he was able to open his own place.

César told his stories with plenty of details, some rather irrelevant—like his many one-night stands with his dance students—and laughed out loud at his own fecklessness.

He was telling us about an affair with a married woman when Professor Rodrigues arrived.

Sorry I'm late. He wiped the sweat from his forehead with a napkin; no doubt he had come running.

No problem, Prof, César said. I've kept them entertained with stories from my good old days.

Miryam sends her apologies, Professor, I said. She had to attend a last-minute meeting with the lawyers.

I understand, Rodrigues said. I trust you'll tell her about our talk today. But no recording devices, OK?

Sure. This is my friend Elena Ruggiero. Unfortunately, she doesn't speak our language well.

My pleasure, Rodrigues said, and shook her hand and smiled.

I want to get right to the point, he said in his vaguely Australian accent. I've been digging a little deeper into the chamber of commerce files about the travel agency Miryam mentioned at our meeting the other day, and I've realized that you and I are on parallel paths. It's interesting how things turn out. We're all setting the pieces of a puzzle in our own way, looking here and there, at places we know or are able to see.

What do you mean, Professor?

Apologies. I'm rambling a little, he said. I just

came from searching archives, and I'm a bit tired. The business group that owned the company that brought employees from Thailand is the one that owns or owned the travel agency that you are investigating in Macau. It looked like two different groups until the year 2000 when they merged, even though the principals were practically the same. It took me a while to make sure because, as I said before, we have limited access to the archives of the chambers of commerce. For the time being, I don't know how this is going to influence your work, but in my case this finding is good evidence that could establish a direct relationship between the trafficking of women of the last three decades with the system of forced prostitution of the Imperial Japanese Army during the war. The link is the Thai subsidiary. At some point, it was managed by a former officer of the army, who we believe was involved with one of the infamous comfort-women stations in Singapore. Interestingly enough, some of the pieces of the puzzle came to me by pure coincidence, although now that I think about it, there were clues, but I couldn't or didn't want to see them. Rodrigues stopped abruptly and looked out at the street; we were sitting by the window, and it was starting to rain. By the way, he said after a moment, his gaze on us once again. How is the investigation of the travel agency going?

Not very well, Professor. I recounted the meeting

with Tariba and the other lawyers the best I could.

So they must hire other lawyers, Elena said.

Which will delay the proceedings, Rodrigues added.

It looks that way, I said.

I feel sorry for Miryam that there's yet another obstacle, Rodrigues said. If I had known last year that she was investigating that particular company, we could have collaborated.

That piece of information came to her recently, I said.

I see. The same in my case. The important thing is just that: from now on we should work together. Naomi and I have made good progress on our project with the business groups.

You mentioned a secret society, I said.

Secret society? Rodrigues repeated as if to himself. Ah, yes, he went on. I forgot I mentioned that during our first meeting. We haven't gotten that far, but we see the bigger picture a little better. It's a complicated issue that will take more time. We'll have to start a new research project in Thailand and dig deeper into the Macau archives. In these two years, we've worked together with some lawyers, friends of Naomi, and have concentrated on some of the illegal activities of the business groups that I mentioned before, but mostly in Japan.

We need to go out and do research, like you did in Macau. Unfortunately, our obligations at the university take away a lot of time, not only teaching but administration, which is a nightmare, incidentally. Rodrigues paused and again looked out the window. It was raining harder; from a steady clatter, it went to a loud roar.

It's a hailstorm right now, he said, sounding concerned. Elena and I got up and went to the window. There was already a white layer of hail on the street.

Sorry to jump to another subject, Professor, but I suspect there's something that might interest you. Do you know Javier Pinto?

Of course I do. To him I owe the coincidence I mentioned a moment ago. He was the one who had me dig through the Macau archives. He was investigating something about a Japanese doctor who lived there during the war.

For the book he's writing?

What book?

I understand that he's writing a historical novel about postwar Japan.

I didn't know he was writing a novel, Rodrigues said and laughed. But I'm not surprised. A couple of years ago he published a book of short stories with a local publisher. How do you know him?

I don't actually know him, I said. I met him once,

though. He was the one who recruited Elena in San Francisco to work at the language school.

Ah yes, Javier is a very enterprising man.

César told me that he knows Toro-san.

Rodrigues rubbed his goatee and looked at César for a moment. True, true, he said. I forgot you guys know each other. I wonder who Javier is talking about. Anyway, I've been researching that character. It's a very particular case. It'll seem strange to you, but I think Toro-san is not one man but several, at least two. Let me explain. The Toro-san whom Margarita Rocha briefly met was an older man, say fifty-five to sixty-five. What's curious is that it fits more or less with what my colleague Naomi has heard lately, and with what has been informally reported on that character through testimonies that Naomi has been collecting in the last ten years or so. At that time, I was not aware of that research; I didn't even know Naomi well; I worked in another department of the university. In a statement that Naomi recorded in 1992, for example, when Tony was the best-known trafficker, one of his victims said she had met Tony's boss, an older gentleman, tall and gray-haired with a manly voice, who was also known as Toro-san. More recently, in 2002, a young Colombian woman, whose real name I don't remember, whom Naomi helped a few years ago, said that the man to whom she owed her debt was an older man nicknamed Toro-san, who was tall, with spiky salt-and-pepper hair, whom she had seen fleetingly in the club where she worked.

The man whom everyone knows, but nobody has actually seen, I said as by reflex.

I see you've read the article by Ruiseñor, Javier Pinto's pseudonym, Rodrigues said, with a smile from side to side.

Javier Pinto? Elena asked. I don't understand.

Pinto has a bilingual blog and publishes articles on various topics, I explained.

I didn't know, Elena said and narrowed her eyes.

There's a ten-year age difference, but it could be the same man, César said and crossed his arms. Nowadays, there are cosmetic treatments and plastic surgeries to make you look younger than you are. But they could also be father and son, he added and slapped the table with his hand.

It's possible, Rodrigues said, in a louder voice. The hailstorm continued, and the resulting racket increased in staccato bursts. There's another clue that I just found out about that points in that direction, he went on. A few weeks ago, Miryam copied me in an email addressed to Naomi in which she's asking her to add a man named Ibuke to the list of people you're investigating in the Macau case. I didn't pay much attention to that detail then, but yesterday when I was reviewing the archives of the main business and finance journal in Tokyo with a new search engine that we have at the university, using Toro-san as a keyword, I found an article published in 1990 which mentions a man named Ibuke, nicknamed Toro-san, who was a partner in a company suspected of promoting sex tourism in Thailand at the time. Guess what the man who appears in the photograph that goes with the article looks like.

Middle-aged, with gray, somewhat bristling hair, César said and smiled smugly.

Indeed! Rodrigues shouted, as if the answer deserved a prize. Although the quality of the photo is very bad, he said. It could be a slightly younger man, between forty and fifty years old; his features are blurred.

Was he arrested? César asked.

The article said that for the moment, there was no concrete evidence, but that the police and the Ministry of Trade were investigating, Rodrigues replied.

So, Ibuke could be Toro-san? I asked, and I looked at Elena whose face had reddened.

It's possible, but not likely. You have to remember that this article came out in 1990. What's possible is what César suggested, that is, that the Toro-san that Margarita Rocha saw is the son of Toro-san from the article I just mentioned, the one named Ibuke. Rodrigues paused to drink some of the tea that the waitress had served us.

The samurai, I said, again almost by reflex.

What did you say? Rodrigues asked.

I'm sorry Professor. It's a long story. Don't mind me; please continue. I looked at Elena, who looked puzzled. She rubbed her temples with her fingers as when a headache struck her.

What you said is interesting, Ricardo, Rodrigues went on. There's a famous samurai with that surname, who participated in a revolt against the imperial Meiji government. It'd be odd if the Ibuke of the article were from the same line, the same family. Even more so if that Ibuke is Toro-san's father, the one whom Margarita Rocha met. Odd but unlikely. But we can't rule anything out. Sometimes reality surpasses fiction…

NINE

I woke up and felt serene and light, as if during the night, I had recovered from an affliction that had befallen me without my being aware of it. I had not felt anything like this for some time, perhaps since the day I decided that I would not go home; it would be almost two years, during which my life had completely changed.

A dim light bathed the room; I had forgotten to close the thick curtains before I went to sleep. It was only five o'clock in the morning on the digital clock on the bedside table; I had awakened at dawn, as it oddly happened during the holidays, just when I didn't have to worry about oversleeping. I stretched my arms and legs. Last night's walk had done me good; it had relaxed my body and cleared my mind. I had gone aimlessly along the main avenue for several blocks beyond Roppongi crossing, and then had wandered around a neighboring residential area of narrow lanes. It had been raining lightly, as when we had returned to the hotel from César's bar, but rather than a nuisance, it had felt comforting, it had brought back childhood memories in my grandparents' village in a temperate area, where such a fine drizzle often fell in the mornings.

Elena muttered something I did not understand, perhaps she was speaking in her sleep.

What time is it?

Five-fifteen, I said.

It can't be, she said.

You slept more than ten hours. Are you feeling OK?

At what time did we go to bed?

You at seven; me at around midnight.

I told you not to let me sleep that long.

I tried to wake you, but you told me to leave you alone.

We didn't see Lisa and Veronique…

Don't worry. I told them you were resting.

Did they call?

Veronique. First to your mobile, then to mine. You didn't even flinch. We'll see them tonight. Veronique is going to make one of her famous dinners.

And Lydia and Felipe?

We'll see them tonight too. They told me to give you a hug.

Elena sat on the bed and rubbed her eyes. I've got to call my mom, she said.

Are you going to tell her everything?

Not all. Well, I really don't know what to tell her. Perhaps just that my father no longer lives in Japan, and that nobody knows anything about him. You've got to help me think what to say.

Are you going to lie to her?

Remember that we're not sure of anything.

I think it's hard for you to accept the possibility, now nearly at one hundred percent, that Ibuke-san is a real crook.

Don't be so sure of what I think. Don't think it had not occurred to me that it would be so. I was used to thinking that because it's what my mom always told me. I was hoping she was wrong, but now with what Tariba told you and what Professor Rodrigues told us, I realize that it's most likely so. What hurts me the most is that I may never know.

Don't you think it would be better to tell her everything?

No, Ricardo. I know my mother well. I think she would be even more disappointed. I think she's always secretly wished that my father wasn't at all like she suspected. I now realize that her insistence that I don't look for him was partly to protect herself.

I don't know what to tell you, I said.

Elena looked at me and put her hands to her face.

Maybe you are right. I've got to think this through. I'll call tomorrow.

If we confirm our suspicions, will you go back to San Francisco?

I don't think so, she said in a small voice, and looked at me in the eye. It may seem crazy to you, but more than ever, I feel that I have to be here, at least for a while. My connection to Japan is not just because of my father. Maybe it never was. Maybe it was just an excuse to run away and experience something different that in some way is also mine.

I think I understand what you mean. An image of my parents came unexpectedly for an instant to my mind. We're going back tomorrow, I added.

What? Why so soon?

A few things happened while you were sleeping. After Veronique, Miryam called to tell me that she had changed our return to tomorrow afternoon. She said that our priority from now on was to work on a proposal to open a branch office in Tokyo. I already told you that that's what Miryam talked about with the other lawyers over the phone at Tariba's office.

Could you work in Tokyo?

I don't know. It depends on several things. This afternoon we have a meeting with Miryam's Japanese lawyer friends, where she'll propose that they merge with our firm. It seems that they had talked about it before, though informally. If they agree, Miryam would come to Tokyo right away. She says that I could do all my internships in the new office, so I could come during the summers. Plus, there's the possibility of an exchange program, if I get into Berkeley Law.

There is something that doesn't work in your story, Ricardo. You sound enthusiastic. I don't recognize you.

You're right, I said. I'm a changed man.

Stop joking. That's excellent news, she shouted, and gave me a hug that almost kicked me out of bed. Although it makes me sad that you're leaving so soon, she said.

Just when I was getting used to this.

What else happened? Elena asked and fixed her bangs with her hand.

I went out for a walk and almost got lost.

Did you go alone?

I couldn't sleep. I thought I'd go to César's bar, but I wasn't in the mood.

You could have talked to Felipe.

I did talk to him. He called me, and we talked for a bit while I walked.

That's why you almost got lost.

He said he was thinking of working with César.

I already knew. He's had that idea ever since he met him.

You don't think it's a good idea?

I don't know. You know he didn't make a good impression on me. Besides, with all the stuff about my father, I haven't had any time to think about anything else.

I hear you. He'll tell us tonight.

How is it that you almost got lost?

I walked on a long street around the new buildings where you said there was a concert hall. It was all dark out there; I thought I was in a ghost town. When I came back to the avenue, I felt a bit disoriented; I didn't know which way the hotel was. I was going to check with the GPS in my mobile, when I realized that I was in front of a black stone sculpture: a square mass with an egg-shaped hole with its apex, in the upper right corner, which seemed to tilt in that direction, as if it were some sort of creature moving very slowly.

Did you see it moving?

No; I meant that I thought it was moving. Don't think I'm crazy, but I stared at the sculpture for a long while. I was attracted to it in some visceral way I can't explain in words. I was enthralled watching the raindrops sliding down the smooth, shiny stone surface…

You're definitely weird today, Ricardo, interrupted

Elena. You sound like you've had a hallucination.

Or maybe an epiphany.

What do you mean?

Never mind. I don't know how to explain it to you right now.

Speaking of time, I've got to run home to change, and prepare a lesson. I have a class at eight, a new course. Call me at noon, OK?

The meeting with the lawyers went on until the early evening. To my surprise, Ramos, the Colombian consul, and Professors Rodrigues and Takeyama were there. Joining our team were also two other paralegals, including Shigeru, the young Japanese guy whom I had not seen since San Francisco; he was staying at some relatives' house and had not come by our hotel. My job consisted of drafting the minutes of the meeting, which would help Miryam prepare the formal proposal for the merger. Fortunately, we also did a video recording of the meeting to show the other partners of the firm and help me edit the minutes.

There were several surprises, one of which was somewhat embarrassing for Miryam and her Japanese colleagues, when Professor Rodrigues spoke of how relatively easy it had been for him to establish the link between the Macau case, the sex tourism business in Thailand, and the trafficking of women in Japan. It was also a bit of a dull moment because Rodrigues expanded on the comfort women system during World War II, a topic Miryam and one of the Japanese lawyers knew well enough to ask each other questions, which momentarily turned the meeting into a kind of academic symposium.

The other surprise was the news about Margarita Rocha. Ramos said that she told him she was going on holiday to Singapore for a week, and then would go on to Dubai, where she had apparently been offered a job at a public relations agency. The latter confused some of the Japanese lawyers who didn't understand what a public relations agency was. Our Japanese paralegal had to explain with several examples—apparently not very relevant—that made some of the lawyers laugh, although I don't know why. By the way Ramos looked during the discussion on public relations—all in English but peppered with Japanese words—I got the impression that he was disappointed by Margarita's decision; perhaps he liked her and had imagined he could have helped her in some other way.

There was also a surprise for me: to be part of the Tokyo team, I would have to learn Japanese, and begin an intensive course immediately after taking the LSAT, which meant that I would have time for nothing more than studying in the next four to five years. Despite that, I felt a little euphoric with the idea that my life was taking a firm course. It remained to be seen whether I could accomplish what was expected of me.

At the end of the meeting, there was talk of the lawsuit Miryam was going to file in a San Francisco court. One of the Japanese lawyers said that it was a good idea, but that he thought it would be better to wait a few months until they had the opportunity to study the case in depth, to see whether they could make it more compelling. Miryam's lawyer friend who specialized in human rights law said that with the new information they had about Ibuke-san—whether he was one or more people, father and son—they could now dig deeper into the local archives. They all agreed that they would have to think very hard about how to get Ibuke out of Thailand. According to the initial investigations of the detectives they hired, Ibuke was married to a Thai woman from a very important family in Bangkok with ties in political circles and the royal court, and had two teenage daughters.

I arrived at Elena's building in a taxi, almost three-quarters of an hour late. The weather was still foul: it was very windy, and it was raining much harder than I expected. The taxi driver must have guessed that I was worried, so he reassured me that the weather was typical of the yearly monsoon, and that there were rarely ever any accidents or mishaps in the city.

Felipe opened the door and gave me a tight hug. The apartment looked different: it was lit differently, more subdued and cozy. There were candles everywhere, and from the kitchen came a pleasant smell of spices.

We're going to miss you again, Felipe said.

I hope to be back soon, in four or five months.

Elena told us, Lisa said. Are they going to help you with law school tuition?

Yes, although we haven't discussed it in detail. I have to take the exam next month, decide where to apply, and wait until I get accepted. It's a long way off.

And when you graduate, would you come to Tokyo permanently?

I don't know. If you are still here, of course.

I'm not going back to the United States, Felipe said. I couldn't with the new government. As I told you last night, I'm going to work with César, also with Javier Pinto. The idea is to set up another restaurant, which at the same time would be a Latin American cultural center, he added. We would offer Spanish and Portuguese courses; cooking classes, Mexican and Peruvian, to begin with; and dancing lessons, of course.

What does Javier Pinto have to do? Elena asked.

Felipe had a sip of his wine before answering.

When we talked about it for the first time at César's bar, Javier said that he could help us organize the cultural calendar. It seems that he has several journalist friends who work in cultural projects, and officers at Latin American embassies and consulates. He said he could also contribute a sum of money to become a minority shareholder.

It's a plan for now, added Lydia, who came from the kitchen with Veronique and Elena.

I'm going to help them, said Veronique. Lisa and I are going to Mexico this winter during the end-of-year holidays, and we will take classes in Oaxacan folk cuisine.

All very good ideas, Elena said and made a skeptical face. We'll see if you see them through. For now, let's sit down to dinner. Veronique and Lisa had been in and out of the kitchen. They served a chicken stew with brown rice.

Ricardo had an epiphany looking at your favorite sculpture, Elena said while we ate, looking at Veronique.

Oh yeah? Geniuses think alike. She laughed. I'm very attracted to that piece. I don't know why, though. I just like to look at it. Maybe it's the way it shines. It's in front of the store where I buy my flowers. The ones that Elena arranges to her ikebana style, although I don't know how they are to the traditional Japanese style. Elena is a little rebellious, she added, and pointed to the arrangement of geraniums and carnations in a ceramic vase over the dining-room cabinet. There were four flowers cut at different heights, with a spring of pine in the middle.

Ricardo, tell us about the epiphany, Lydia asked. She seemed a little impatient; talk about art and decor always bored her.

I wouldn't say it was an epiphany, I said. The word has a religious tint, like a revelation. It was more like a moment of sudden mental clarity, where I felt that I was beginning to understand things that before had seemed distant and undefined.

The transformative power of art, Elena ventured.

Perhaps, I replied, but it was not so much an artistic experience. I don't know how to explain it. It was more like beginning to see, like going from darkness to light. I suddenly remembered a movie scene I had seen a long time ago. Like *The Green Ray*, Eric Rohmer's movie.

The one based on the Jules Verne novel? Veronique asked.

I think the idea comes from there, but I don't know if it's true to that text, I said. I think it's mentioned in the script. If I'm not mistaken, in the movie the protagonist sees that ray, an optical phenomenon that is sometimes visible in the precise moment when the sun sets, and begins to realize many things. Who she is and where she's going, who her friends are.

Let's toast to the green ray then, invited Veronique. She raised her glass.

Roppongi Crossing

The last time I was at the Roppongi crossing in 2007, I was not waiting for anyone like I had before many times when I lived and worked in Tokyo. I was just passing through, on my way to an evening lecture at the university where I had been invited as a visiting researcher for a few months. I was about to cross, when I was struck with sudden nostalgia. To my mind came flashing memories of the many people I had met at that spot, journalists, academics, friends, and the places we had gone for dinner or a drink in that entertainment district, and the things we had talked about. I decided for the moment to take a step back, and joined the small crowd gathered there, for no other reason than to indulge in memories of things long past.

As I was looking for the right spot to stand that would give me a panoramic view, I saw, a few paces away, a man of Mediterranean or Levantine looks, who seemed familiar. I got a little closer to him, and had the odd and startling feeling that I was looking at me a few years ago, when I still sported a full beard and had a little more hair on my head. The resemblance was uncanny. I felt queasy in my stomach. As I looked at his features, and the way he stood: slightly hunched as I do sometimes when I am worried about something, it occurred to me that the only sensible explanation was that this man was either my doppelgänger or an alternative me, who by accident of the universe had remained in Tokyo, and had a life I was not aware of. The man was looking at a fixed point on the other side of the crossing, as if he were meditating or in a trance. I came a little closer still, with apprehension, fearful of how he would react, and realized with great relief, that it was someone I knew or had met years ago, though I could not remember how or where, much less his name.

I retreated to my original waiting spot, feeling a little shaken up, and dug into my memories of people I had met in the past who could, given the passage of time, have turned up to look like me a few years ago. It was to no avail; my mind drew a complete blank. In the meantime, the man kept on looking impassively at the other side, his body perfectly still. I thought about going up and talking to him, but I could not muster the courage to do it. Suddenly, he looked at his watch and started to walk towards the edge of the crossing. As if by instinct, I raised my hand, meaning to catch his attention. I meant to say something but no words came to my mouth. The man looked at me for an instant, then to the other side, as if he had understood that I had raised my hand to get the attention of someone to his left, and then hurriedly crossed the street. I tried to follow him but I was detained by the traffic light. By the time I made it to the other side, I could no longer see him. I ran in one direction and the other but he was nowhere to be found. After a few frantic minutes, I abandoned the search. I felt angered and relieved in equal measure. My hesitation, my worst trait, had again prevented me from acting on instinct, or perhaps saved me from the embarrassment of being far off the mark, if not completely deluded.

By sheer coincidence, if you can believe that at this point in my story, I saw the man again a few days later, and much to my surprise at the university, in the very conference room where I was presenting a paper about my recent research. Luckily, I had not seen him in the audience. I would have probably had a panic attack. After I finished, he came over to ask a question, and I immediately remembered I had met him at least twenty years before on a trip to India. From the way he asked the question, I deduced that he was also a historian. You really don't remember me, I said and looked him in the eye. I don't think we have ever met, he replied;

but then looked back at me with a grimace of doubt, and apologized. He said he did not have a good memory for faces. I told him we had met in a small hamlet in Goa, at a restaurant on a shack on the beach, where they served the most amazing dishes of the local cuisine. We had dinner together, I reminded him. One evening there was no other free table facing the sea and you asked me if you could join me. After dinner, we drank coffee-flavored *feni,* and talked about the Portuguese in India. We had both recently visited the nearby *Aguada* Fort, built in the sixteenth century. At some point, an older European woman, French, if I remember correctly, who had been sitting next to us, perhaps even listening to our conversation, came to our table and point blank asked us whether we had read Antonio Tabucchi's *Indian Nocturne.* We both said no, and then to our astonishment she produced the book, which she must have been reading until recently, left it on the table and said that we *should* read it, that she was sure we would like it or find it useful, and then, making a kind of a bow, a strange gesture, I remember thinking, she took her leave. I have that book in my library, he told me, but it came to me in a completely different way. As for the dinner in Goa, I remember the place you mentioned, but I don't remember meeting anyone there.

That night we did not speak again, the head of the department of Latin American Studies at the university invited us to dinner and we sat at opposite ends of the table.

The following day, I ran into him at the university library, around noon, and he invited me to lunch. I was intrigued by our meeting, he said after we ordered. Last night, as I was reviewing a text that I am writing, I realized that perhaps you were right and that we had met before. I am at a kind of crossroads with several writing projects, you see, he added, the most urgent and personal of which is a novel where I tell the story of a woman, very dear to me with whom I shared many things, and with whom I regrettably parted ways, and never saw again, though I thought I did, mistakenly, in Goa, of all places, a couple of years ago. Because the book is also about me looking for her, I have added fictional events to explain things that happen in the text or to fill up gaps in the plot. I am therefore no longer sure whether I can trust my recollections, which have by now fused with the recollections of the characters in the novel…

I am sorry I did not pay attention to you at Roppongi Crossing the other day, he continued after a short pause. I did, in fact, see that you raised your hand, and understood that you wanted to talk to me, but for some reason I felt afraid, like I had seen a ghost, and hurried across the street. I know it sounds irrational, but sometimes I react in bizarre ways when something takes me by surprise… That evening, he went on, I was on my way to see some friends and colleagues to tell them about something important I found in the local archives, something that would matter to many people, a piece of a puzzle, so to speak. But just like what you told me happened to you that afternoon —an interesting coincidence, by the way— I was suddenly taken by a wave of nostalgia. In my case, of the times I had met the woman I mentioned before at the crossing, including the last evening we spent together.

He made as if he was going to continue talking, even lifted his finger as if about to point something out, but changed his mind and held back. He probably realized that to continue, he would have to take the thread of other stories, of other lives, and that would mean opening other doors and following other paths. I waited a few instants before speaking and told him that I understood, and for the first time in a long while, I felt that I did.

can be obtained
om